2

DATE DUE

APR 1 1 2009	

DEMCO, INC. 38-2931

Muse of Fire

MUSE OF FIRE

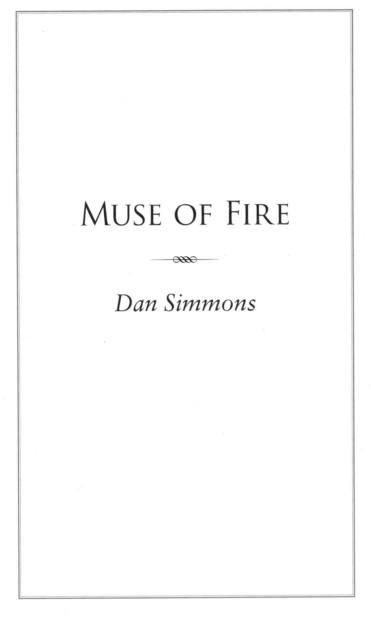

Dan Simmons

Subterranean Press 2008

First Edition

ISBN
978-1-59606-181-1

Subterranean Press
PO Box 190106
Burton, MI 48519

www.subterraneanpress.com

First appeared in *The New Space Opera*, edited by Gardner Dozois
and Jonathan Strahan.

F
SIM

I SOMETIMES THINK THAT none of the rest of the things would have happened if we hadn't performed the Scottish Play that night at Mezel-Goull. Nothing good ever comes from putting on the Scottish Play—if we remember any history at all, we know that—and much bad often does.

But I doubt if there have ever been ramifications like this before.

The *Muse of Fire* followed the Archon funeral barge out of the Pleroma into the Kenoma, slipped out of its pleromic wake like a newborn emerging from a caul, and made its own weak-fusion way to our next stop on the tour, a world known only as 25-25-261B. I'd been there before. By this time, I'd been with the Earth's Men long enough to have visited all of the four hundred or so worlds we were allowed to tour regularly. They say that there are over ten thousand worlds in the Tell—ten thousand we humans have been scattered to, I mean—but I'll never know if that's true. *We'll* never know.

I always love the way the *Muse* roars down through cloud and sky on her thundering three-mile-long pillar of fire, especially at night, and the descent to the arbeiter community on the coastal plateau below the Archon keep of Mezel-Goull was no disappointment.

We landed on the inner edge of the great stone shelf separating the human villages from the acid-tossed sea cliffs. One glance at the *Muse*'s log had reminded me that 25–25–261B had only three variations in its day and weather: twilight-bright dimness and scalding spray blown in by winds from the crashing black ocean of sulfuric acid for fourteen hours each day; twilight-bright dimness and sandstorms blown to the barely habitable coasts by hot winds from the interior of the continent for another fourteen hours each day; and full darkness when no winds blew for the final fourteen hours. The air was breathable here—all of our tour worlds had that in common, of course, since we only travel to planets where the Archons keep arbeiter and dole slaves—but even in the middle of their twenty-one hours of daytime on this bleak rock, the sky brightened to only a dim, brooding grayness because of the constant layers of clouds, and no one ventured out unprotected during the hours when the scalding spray blew in from the black, sulfuric sea.

The *Muse* touched down during the hours the hot *simoom* winds blew. No one came out from the huddled stone city to meet us. The thousands of arbeiters were either sleeping in their barracks between shifts or working in the mines, dropping down to darkness in rusty buckets and then following veins miles deeper underground to harvest a gray fungus that the Archons considered a delicacy. The few hundred local doles in their somewhat higher huddle of stone hovels were doing whatever doles do: recording, accounting, measuring, file-keeping, waiting for instructions from their masters via the dragomen.

We stayed inside the ship while the hot winds roared, but the *Muse*'s cabiri scrambled out through maintenance hatches like so many flesh-and-metal spiders, opened storage panels, rigged worklights, strung long cables from the hull, pounded k-chrome stakes into solid rock, unfolded steelmesh canvas, and had the main performance tent up and rigidified within thirty minutes. The first show was not scheduled to begin for another six hours, but it took a while for the cabiri to arrange the lighting and stage and set up the many rows of seats. The old Globe Theater in London during the Bard's time, according to troupe lore, would seat three thousand, but our little tent-theater comfortably seated about eight hundred human beings. We expected far fewer than that during each of our four scheduled performances on 25–25–261B.

On many worlds we have permission to land at a variety of arbeiter huddles, but this world had only this single major human population center. The town has no name, of course. We humans gave up naming things long ago, abandoning that habit along with our culture, politics, arts, history, hope, and sense of self. No one in the troupe or among the arbeiters and doles here had a clue as to who had named the Archon keep Mezel-Goull, which apparently meant "Devil's Rest," but the name seemed appropriate. It *sounded* appropriate, even if the words actually had no meaning.

The hulking mass of Archon steel and black stone dominated an overhanging cliff about six miles north of this plateau upon which the humans were housed. Through binoculars, I could see the tall slits of tower windows glowing yellow while pale white searchlights stabbed out from the keep and up to the highlands, then probed down over the human escarpment and across the *Muse*, then swept out to the sulfur sea. None of us from the troupe had ever been to the keep, of course—why would humans, other than dragomen (whom most of us do not consider human), have any business with Archons? They own us, they control our lives, they dictate our actions and fates, but they have no interest in us and we usually return the favor.

⁂

THERE WERE TWENTY-THREE of us in this Shakespearean troupe called the Earth's Men. Not all of us were men, of course, although we knew through stage history that in the Bard's day even the women's roles were acted by males.

My name is Wilbr. I was twenty SEY old that day we landed on 25–25–261B and had been chosen for the troupe when I was nine and turned out to be good enough at memorizing my lines and hitting my marks to be on stage for most productions, but by age twenty I knew in my heart that I would never be a great actor. Probably not even a good one. But my hope remained to play Hamlet someday, somehow, somewhere. Even if only once.

There were a couple of others about my age in the Earth's Men; Philp was one of them and a good friend. There were several young women in the troupe, including Aglaé, the best and most attractive Juliet and Rosalind I've ever seen: she was a year older than me and my choice for girlfriend, lover, and wife, but she never noticed me;

Tooley was our age, but he primarily did basic maintenance engineering on the *Muse*, although he could hold a spear in a crowd scene if pressed to.

Kemp and Burbank were the two real leaders of the troupe, along with Kemp's wife (and Burbank's lover) Condella, whom everyone secretly, and never affectionately, referred to as "the Cunt." I never learned how the nickname got started—some say it was her French accent as Catherine talking to her maid in *Henry V*—but other and less kind guesses would probably have been equally accurate.

Kemp had always been a clown in the most honorable sense of the word: a young arbeiter comic actor and improviser when he was chosen for the Earth's Men by Burbank's father, the former leader of the troupe, more than fifty years earlier. One of Kemp's specialties was Falstaff although he'd lost weight as he aged, so he now had to wear a special suit fitted out with padding whenever he played Sir John. He was a brilliant Falstaff, but he was even more brilliant—frighteningly so—as Lear. If Kemp had had his way, we would have performed *The Tragedy of King Lear* for every second performance.

Burbank had the weight for Falstaff but not the comic timing, and since he was in his early fifties SEY, was not quite old enough—nor impressive enough in personality—to make an adequate Lear. Yet he was now too old to play Hamlet, the role his father had owned and in which this younger Burbank had also excelled. There was something about the Prince's dithering and indecisiveness and self-pity that perfectly fit Burbank. Still, it was a frustrating time for Burbank and he marked it by getting hammier and hammier in the roles Kemp allowed him and by screwing Kemp's much younger wife every chance he got.

Alleyn was our young Hamlet now and a wonderful one at that, especially when set against Burbank's Claudius and Kemp's Polonius. For villains we had Heminges. Kemp once said to me after a few drinks that our real Heminges out-Iagoes Iago on and off the stage. He also said that he wished that Heminges had Richard III's hump and personality just so things would be more peaceful aboard the *Muse*.

Coeke was our Othello and was perfect in the role for more reasons than his skin color. Recca, especially adept at playing Kate the Shrew, was Heminges's wife and Coeke's mistress—when she felt like it—and her easy infidelity had done little in recent years to improve Heminges's personality.

Heminges was also our only revolutionary.

I should explain that.

There were a few men or women out of the billions scattered among the Archon and other alien stars who believed that humans should revolt, throw off the yoke of the Archons and reestablish the "human era." As if that were possible. They were all cranks and malcontents like Heminges.

I was about fifteen and we were in transit in the Pleroma when I first heard Heminges mutter his suicidal sedition.

"How could we possibly 'rise up' against the Archons?" I asked. "Humans have no weapons."

Heminges had given me his Iago smile. "We're *in* the most powerful weapon left to our species, young Master Wilbr."

"The *Muse*?" I said stupidly. "How could the *Muse* be a weapon?"

Heminges had shaken his handsome head in something like disgust. "The touring ships are the last artifacts left from the human age of greatness," he hissed at me. "Think of it, Wilbr...three fusion reactors, a fusion engine that used to move our ancestors around the Earth's solar system in *days* and which the Archon cabiri bots...and Tooley...keep tuned for us. Why, the flame tail from this ship is three miles long during early atmosphere entry."

The words had made me cold all through. "Use the *Muse* as a weapon?" I said. "That's..." I had no words for it. "The Archons would catch us and put us in a pain synthesizer for the rest of our lives." I assumed this last statement would put an end to the discussion.

Kemp had told me about the Archons' pain synthesizers the first months I'd been with the troupe. The lowest of the four tiers of alien races rarely deigned to deal with us, but when dole or arbeiter disappointed them or disobeyed them in any way, the Archons dropped the hapless people into a pain synthesizer and kept them alive for extra decades. The settings on the synthesizers were reputed to include such pleasures as "crushed testicle" or "hot poker up the anus" or "blade through eyeball"...and the pain never ended. Drugs in the synthesizer soup kept the prisoner awake and suffering for long decades. And, Kemp had whispered to me, the first thing the Archons do to someone going into the pain synthesizer is to remove their tongue and vocal cords so they cannot scream.

Heminges laughed. "To punish us, the Archon would have to be alive. And so would we. Three fusion reactors make for a very nice bomb, young Master Wilbr."

That thought had kept me awake for weeks, but when I asked Tooley, who was apprenticing with Yerick who was then the ship's engineer, if such a thing were possible, he told me that it wasn't—really—that the reactors could melt and that would be messy, but that they couldn't be turned into what he called "a fusion bomb." Not really. Besides, Tooley said in his friendly lisp, the Archons had long since retrofitted *Muse* with so many of their own posttech safeguards and monitors that no amount of mere human tinkering could cause the reactors to go critical.

"What would we do if we...did...somehow attack the Archons?" I asked Heminges when I was fifteen. "Where would we go? Humans can't transit the Pleroma...only Abraxas can do that, praise be unto His name, and He shares those sacred secrets only with the *Demiurgos*, Poimen, and Archons. We'd be stranded forever in whatever star system we'd started the revolt in."

Heminges had only snorted at that and turned his attention back to his ale.

Still...all these years later...just the thought of losing the *Muse* made me shiver. She was home to me. She was the only home I'd known in the past eleven SEY and I fully expected to call her home for another fifty SEY until it was time for me to be carted back to Earth on a funeral barge.

WE WERE PERFORMING *Much Ado About Nothing* and because I was playing Balthasar, Don Pedro's attendant, I didn't have to go with the supernumeraries as they went out to drum up business with the Circus Parade.

There were twenty cabiri for every human from our troupe, but the parade is hard to ignore. Those not preparing for major roles in *Much Ado* and our huge metal spiders made their way to the dole city on the higher ridges before the cabiri activated their holograms and my friends already in costume began blowing their horns and shouting and singing into their loudhailers.

Only a few doles joined the procession then—they rarely turn out for the Circus Parade—but by the time the line of brightly costumed actors and the procession of free-roaming elephants with red streamers, tigers, dromedaries carrying monkeys wearing fezzes, wolves in purple robes, and even some leaping dolphins got halfway through the arbeiter city, there were several hundred people following them back to the *Muse*.

More trumpets and announcements began blaring from the ship herself. The lower hull is always part of the stage and backdrop, of course, and this night the *Muse* extruded her lower balconies and catwalks and rows of spots and other lights beneath the tent just minutes before the crowd arrived. Holograms and smart paint became the fields and forests and hilltop manse of Leonato while we players in the wings hurried with our last costume and makeup preparations.

We started on time to a final flourish of silencing trumpets. Peering out from behind the arras like Polonius, I could see that there were about six hundred paying customers in their seats. (The chinks were only good in pubs and the few provision outlets, of course, but they were good on all the worlds we visited. Chinks are chinks.)

In the old days, *Much Ado* would have been Kemp's and Condella's tour de force, but a middle-aged Benedick and Beatrice simply didn't work, so after watching Burbank and Recca being merely adequate—and both very bitchy—in the roles for years, on this tour Alleyn and Aglaé were playing the leads.

They were amazing. Alleyn brought to Benedick all the bravado and uncertainty of the sexually experienced young nobleman who remained terrified of love and marriage. But it was Aglaé who dominated the performances—just as the real Beatrice dominated Leonato's compound above Messina with her incomparable and almost frightening wit leavened by a certain hint of a disappointed lover's melancholy. Someone once said that of all of Shakespeare's characters, it was Beatrice and Benedick that one would most want to be seated next to at a dinner party, and I confess that it was a pleasure being onstage with these two consummate young actors in those roles.

Kemp had to satisfy himself with a scene-stealing turn as Dogberry, Burbank blustered as Leonato, and Heminges had to throttle down his ultimate Iago evil to fit into the lesser villain of Don John, a character that Kemp once suggested to me was indeed Shakespeare's early, rough sketch for Iago. Anne played the hapless Hero and Condella was reduced to overacting as Margaret, Hero's waiting gentlewoman attendant. (Condella always created precisely the character here in *Much Ado* that she used for the Nurse in *Romeo and Juliet*, even though I'm certain that the Bard hadn't meant for the two to have any similarities.) And I got to woo her onstage even though I'm twenty SEY younger than she is.

~≋~

THE AUDIENCE, MOSTLY arbeiters in their brown rawool and a few score doles in their cotton gray, laughed hard and applauded and cheered frequently.

Alleyn and Aglaé were wonderful in their act 1 banter and we'd just gotten into act 2 with Benedick asking me to sing a "divine air"—I don't believe I mentioned that they had me play Balthasar primarily because I was the best singer in the troupe now that Davin had died and left us—and I'd just begun the song when everything changed forever.

> *Sigh no more, ladies, sigh no more,*
> *Men were deceivers ever,*
> *One foot in sea, and one on shore,*
> *To one thing constant never.*
> *Then sigh not so, but let them go,*
> *And be you blithe and bonny,*
> *Converting all your sounds of woe*
> *Into Hey, nonny nonny.*

In the middle of my song, into the tent floated a forty-foot-long heavy iron-gray gravity sledge carrying at least eight carapace-hooded, chitinous, four-armed, ten-foot-tall Archons, each sitting deep in its own iron-gray metal throne. Hanging from the sledge by their synaptic fiberneural filaments, which ran down to their hairless, distended skulls like slim, translucent copper hair, were four naked drago-men. Their oversized, lidless eyes focused on the stage and their cartilage-free ears rotating the better to pick up—and relay to their Archon masters—my singing.

Arbeiters and doles created a racket scrambling out of their seats to get out from under the massive, flat-bottomed gravity sledge. Archons landed their vehicles when and where they pleased and more than a few humans from 25–25–261B certainly had been crushed before this night.

But the sledge did not land. It rose to a point just below the tent roof about forty feet from the stage and hovered there. The doles and arbeiters who'd fled found places to sit in the aisles out from under the sledge's shadow and the dangling bare feet of the dragomen and returned their attention to the stage, their faces pale but attentive.

I'm a professional. I did not miss a beat or drop a note. But I know my voice quavered as I sang the next stanza.

Sing no more ditties, sing no more,
Of dumps so dull and heavy.
The fraud of men was ever so,
Since summer first was leavy.
Then sigh not so, but let them go,
And be you blithe and bonny,
Converting all your sounds of woe
Into Hey, nonny nonny.

Gough, playing Don Pedro, did not miss a beat. " 'By my troth, a good song,' " he cried, his eyes never shifting to the sledge and Archons.

"'And an ill singer, my lord,'" was my response. For once I was telling the truth. My voice had cracked or quavered half a dozen times in those eight simple lines of singing.

"'Ha, no, no, faith,'" bellowed Gough/Don Pedro, "'thou sing'st well enough for a shift.'"

My hands were shaking and I *did* sneak a glance at the motionless sledge and the slowly twisting dragomen hanging naked and slick-skinned and hairless and sexless beneath that sledge, the filaments from the four of their skulls running up to red sensory node bundles on the complicated chest carapaces of the eight Archons.

Did the peasant arbeiters and equally peasant doles out there—any of them—have any idea that Gough's use of the ancient word "shift" in his line meant something like "to make do"? Almost certainly not. Almost all of the beauty and subtlety of Shakespeare's language was lost on them. (It had taken me years after the troupe adopted me to begin appreciating it.)

Then what in the hell were the Archons perceiving as they heard these archaic words through the dangling dragomen's ears, saw our colorful costumes and overbright makeup through the dragomen's eyes?

Alleyn caught my eye, forcing my attention back to the play, responded broadly to Don Pedro, and turned to the audience—ignoring the gravity sledge—and gave his chuckling Benedick's reply.

"'An he had been a dog that should have howled thus, they would have hanged him. And I pray God his bad voice bode no mischief. I had as lief have heard the night-raven, come what plague could have come after it.'"

The night-raven, I knew and the arbeiters and doles almost certainly did not know—who in the name of the Gnostic God of All Opposites had any idea what the dragomen and Archons knew?—was the bird of ill omen.

∾

THERE IS ALWAYS a party after a performance. There was that night.

Some worlds are so dolefully awful that we have to hold the party on the *Muse*, inviting the pretty girls and pretty boys aboard (there are no human dignitaries, mayors, burgomasters, commissars, or officials of importance in human life now, only the gray doles, and they don't know how to party). On the more palatable worlds, and 25–25–261B qualified as such, we tried to move the party to a local pub or barn or similar public space. This rock had a pub in the oldest section of arbeiter town. (Those are the only two public institutions that have survived the end of all human politics and culture after our species' hopeless enslavement—pubs and churches. We'd never partied in a church. At least not yet.)

The drinking with the few adventurous arbeiters and storytelling and drinking and gambling and more storytelling and more drinking went on until the sulfur winds began to howl against the titanium shutters, and then the young ones among us began pairing off with the most attractive locals we could cull from the herd.

Aglaé rarely stayed at these parties for long and never went off with locals, but Philp, Pig (our apprentice Pyk), red-haired Kyder, Coeke, Alleyn, Anne, Pope, Lana, the short Hywo, Gough, Tooley, and some of the rest of us each found someone eager to make the beast with two backs with a rare stranger to their world, and two by two, arbeiter and actor, like randy animals filing toward Noah's Ark, we began slipping away from the ebbing party and heading for arbeiters' hovels and barracks and outbuildings and barns.

In my case it was a barn.

We did it three times in the loft that night as the acid rains blew against the stone walls. (It would have been more times, but at age twenty, I'm not as young and resilient as I once was.) The barn held five animals (besides us)—a llama, a cow, a goat, and two chickens. None seemed bothered by our exertions or Larli's loud cries.

Larli was the arbeiter girl who'd invited me home to her barrack's barn. She was fairly typical for a post-performance fling girl: very young but old enough for me not to feel too guilty, curly hair, pretty eyes, broad shoulders, more muscles than I'd ever have, and hands so calloused and strong that several times when I cried out, it was in pain not ecstasy.

She liked to talk and ask questions—also fairly typical for a postplay fling date—and I tried to stay awake and keep up my end of the conversation (since I was too tired to keep anything else up) as the wind and sulfur rain tore at the slate tiles above us.

"You must see a lot of wonderful places," she said, lying back on the blanket on the straw. "Lots of wonderful worlds."

"Uh-huh," I said. I was deciding how to explain that I was going to return to the *Muse* to sleep. I always came home to the *Muse* to sleep after the postperformance. This night was already later than most.

"Have you ever gone to Earth?" she asked. Her voice almost broke on the soft syllable of the last word. They always do.

"I was born on Earth."

I could tell by her silent stare that she didn't believe me.

"A lot of players come from Earth," I said. "I was nine when they chose me."

"There's no one...*alive*...on Earth," she whispered. I could hear the acid rain outside diminish and the hot winds begin to blow. It would not be long before the terminator crossed this plateau. And it was the Sabbath.

I patted her pale but powerfully muscled leg. "There are thousands of living arbeiters on Earth...um...Larli."

"I thought only the dead lived there." She shook her blond curls, flustered. "You know what I mean."

I nodded in the dim glow of one shielded lantern hanging on a post below this loft. "There are a few thousand living humans on Earth," I said quietly. "My family among them. I was born there. The cabiri tend the tombs and do the heavy work, but there is always some labor for the doles and arbeiters."

"What is it like, Wilbr? Earth, I mean? It must be very beautiful."

"It rains a lot," I said. This was an understatement. Earth had not seen a blue sky in more than a thousand years.

"But the oceans...the *perfecti* tell tales of the great blue seas. Oceans of *water*. They must be gorgeous."

"Yes," I said, thinking only of how I was going to disengage myself so I could get back to my bunk on the *Muse*.

The oceans of Earth had been drained by the *Demiurgos* long ago. Everything there now was rock and tombs: metal sarcophagi, tens and hundreds of billions of them, stacked on rocky plains, coastal shelves, deep shadowed mountain ranges that had once been ocean depths. Earth had no ecology, no wild things, no domesticated plants or animals—not even the ubiquitous goats and cows and llamas and chickens and other pathetic livestock scattered among sad arbeiter communities like this around the Tell—and no real towns. The few thousand arbeiters and doles were scattered among the tombs.

"And the sky, so blue," whispered the girl, whose name I'd forgotten again. "It must be *so* lovely."

"Yes," I said and stifled a yawn. My earliest memories were the red skyscars of descending and ascending Archon funeral barges, carrying millions more of freeze-dried human corpses to their resting places and then ascending again with the empty sarcophagi, the massive, ugly ship flames clawing across the gray-clouded sky to the backdrop thunder of their booming pulse drives. The only clear areas on Earth were the spaceports where the funeral barges landed and took off, around the clock, while huge service cabiri unloaded the transport sarcophagi, tumbled the brittle corpses into bins, and then reloaded the containers.

The girl started caressing me again. I gently disengaged her hand and began pulling on my clothes.

"Tomorrow's...today's...Sabbath," I whispered "I'll see you in church."

I ACTUALLY *WAS* religious—I was raised that way—and I did see Larli in church later that morning, but only across the crowded heads of the congregation. I was sure that more doles and arbeiters than usual attended services that day just to see the outworlders. As always, the rough stone pews were filled with the usual bands of brown wool homespun work uniforms, slightly less rough gray cotton administrator tunics, and the small cluster of colorful silks and cottons and wools that we dozen or so regularly churchgoing Earth's Men chose to wear to Mass.

The church itself was no cathedral. The locals had cleaned out one of the stone barns erected by the Archon mechs, put rough glass in the windows, converted the hayloft to a choir loft—my loins stirred when I saw the loft and that's when I searched the crowd for Larli—and put some crude stone and canvas images of Gnostic saints and Abraxas him/herself at stations along the wall and behind the altar rail. The icons and paintings were rough but I could make out Saint Valentinius. Saint Sophia, Saint Thomas, Saint Emerson, Saint Blake, Saint Hesse, Saint Caprocates with his wife Alexandra hovering behind and above him, Saint Menander, Saint Basilides, and Simon Magus. That last prophet of the church was always depicted as flying, and in the painting along the north wall, the painted expression of Simon Magus looked as surprised at his sudden flying ability as the poorly rendered faces of the peasants below him.

Abraxas, of course, held center stage, roughly where a huge cross and Jesus might have hung behind the altar long ago during the brief Christian era. The large sculpture carried the traditional whip and shield—showing the conjoined opposites of attack and defense—and had the usual head of a rooster, body of a man, and legs of heavy, coiled snakes. Behind the sculpture on a black, circular stone backdrop were gold stars with varying number of rays as well as the eight-fold symbol of the *ogdoad*, representing the transcending of the seven planets.

The two *perfecti* at the front of the church—one male, one female, as prescribed by the Abraxic requirement of joining of opposites, one in all white with a black collar band, the other wearing the reverse—performed the opening rituals with the usual provincial blend of ineptitude and enthusiasm.

The male *perfectus* gave the sermon. It was the third sermon from Saint Jung's *Seven Sermons to the Dead* and I could have recited it from memory, and with far more feeling than the white-robed *perfectus* could deliver on his best day. Compared to memorizing and delivering the simplest line from Shakespeare, Jung's rhetoric was baby's work.

The dead approaches like mist out of the swamps and they shouted: "Speak to us further about the highest god!"
—Abraxas is the god whom it is difficult to know. His power is the very greatest because man does not perceive it at all. Man sees the summum bonum, *supreme good, of the sun, and also the* infinum malum, *endless evil, of the devil, but Abraxas, he does not see, for he is undefinable life itself, which is the mother of good and evil alike. Life appears smaller and weaker than the* summum bonum, *wherefore it is hard to think that*

Abraxas should supersede in his power the sun, which is the radiant fountain of all life forces.

Abraxas is the sun and also the eternally gaping abyss of emptiness, of the diminisher and dissembler, the devil.

The power of Abraxas is twofold. You cannot see it, because in your eyes the opposition of this power seems to cancel it out.

That which is spoken by God-the-Sun is life.

That which is spoken by the Devil is death.

Abraxas, however, speaks the venerable and also accursed word, which is life and death at once.

Abraxas generates truth and falsehood, good and evil, light and darkness with the same word and in the same deed. Therefore Abraxas is truly the terrible one.

He is magnificent even as the lion at the very moment when he strikes his prey down. His beauty is like the beauty of a spring morn.

Indeed, he is himself the greater Pan, and also the lesser. He is Priapos.

He is the monster of the underworld, the octopus with a thousand tentacles, he is the twistings of winged serpents and of madness.

He is the hermaphrodite of the lowest beginnings. He is the lord of toads and frogs, who live in water and come out unto the land, and who sing together at high noon and at midnight.

He is fullness, uniting itself with emptiness.

He is the sacred wedding;

He is love and the murder of love;

He is the holy one and his betrayer.
He is the brightest light of day and the deepest
night of madness.
To see him means blindness;
To know him is sickness;
To worship him is death;
To fear him is wisdom;
Not to resist him means liberation.
God lives behind the—

The *perfectus* suddenly fell silent. The priest's gaze was riveted on the rear door of the church and one by one the congregation swiveled their necks to see what or who had interrupted the service.

I'd never seen a dragoman alone and I'd never seen one close up like this. Both new experiences were unsettling.

He—I use the pronoun loosely since dragomen had no sex—was about my height but he had much larger eyes, much larger ears, no lips to speak of, no teeth visible, no real chin, a long tapered nose, and a queerly shaped head, his forehead sloped back along a cranium that seemed to have been malformed rearward until it blended with the long synaptic filaments that trailed on the floor behind now with a faint metallic rustling. His fingers were far too long, as if they had at least one extra joint and perhaps more, and disturbingly spatulate. His feet were flat and too broad—he had no toes and I could hear puckery suckerish sounds as he strode across the broad paving stones of the barn-church. His legs were too long, jointed oddly, and gave the false impression of being almost boneless. He was hairless and naked, of course, and as he passed my pew I saw how his skin glistened wetly, coarsely, like molded wax. He had no nipples. I could see how a waxy fold of loose skin folded down from his lower abdomen to cover whatever orifices he had for urination and excretion; it is common knowledge that dragomen have no real genitals and thus are more *neuter* than hermaphroditic.

He stopped at Kemp's pew and, bending oddly from the waist, leaned toward the leader of our troupe. The dragoman's voice was as high and flat as a young child's without any of a child's charm. "The Heresiarch bids you to perform tonight at the Archon keep. Have your people dressed and prepared for transport at the moment the winds drop on the hour of the third mine shift."

He may have said something else, but if so the words were lost in the explosion of surprised murmuring and shifting in the church.

⤸

"THIS IS OUR chance," whispered Heminges as the men crowded into one of the *Muse*'s two makeup and costuming rooms that afternoon.

"Chance?" said Gough. Kemp and Condella had decided that we were doing the Scottish Play, over Burbank's protests and Alleyn's and Aglaé's indifference.

"To strike," said Heminges. He was costuming himself for the role of Duncan.

Gough rolled his eyes.

"What are you talking about?" I asked. I was already terrified at the thought of performing before the Archons;

I didn't need Heminges's revolution fantasies and conspiracies that night.

"I've never heard of a troupe being invited to perform before Archons before...*in their keep*," whispered Heminges.

"You never heard of it before, because it's never happened before," said Old Adam. He was to be Banquo tonight. His favorite role was as Hamlet's father's ghost. Adam had been to more Bard Rendezvous on Stratford and performed in more competitions there than any of us, even Kemp and Burbank. He knew more lore than anyone else in the Earth's Men.

"Then it *is* perfect," hissed Heminges as he applied his bald wig.

"Perfect for *what*, for Christ's sake? We can't *do* anything up there...but put on the show I mean. If we did...if we did..."

"The pain synthesizers," rumbled Coeke. "For the rest of our lives and then some."

Heminges showed his thin, tight Iago smile. "When we take the *Muse* to the keep, we set thrust to full burn, then take off before—"

"Oh, shut the fuck up, Heminges," said Burbank, who'd come closer without us noticing. "We're not taking the ship up there. The dragoman told Kemp that we were to be fully dressed and have all our props ready by...less than an hour from now...and a gravity sledge is going to take us the six miles to the castle. Do you *really* think the Archons would let us get a weapon...or anything that could be used as a weapon...anywhere near the keep?"

Heminges said nothing.

"I don't want to hear another word of your silly revolution fantasies," snapped Burbank, his voice as mad-strong as Hamlet's speaking to Gertrude. "If you play this particular brand of sick make-believe again—one more word— I swear by Abraxas that we'll leave you behind on this godforsaken rock."

⤜

IT LOOKED AS if two thirds of the arbeiters and doles not at work in the mines showed up to watch us leave on the gravity sledge. It was easy to understand why they were curious. In all the centuries they and their ancestors had been on this rock, the only thing that left from the human city to be taken to the keep were dead bodies to be hauled to the Archon spaceport to await transshipment to Earth.

There was a funeral barge up there now. We'd followed it through the Pleroma to this world and had planned to follow it out in three days to the next planet on our tour.

From the look on the silent arbeiters' faces as we floated past the city and up the road carved into rock toward the highlands, they didn't expect us to return from the keep alive. Perhaps we didn't either. But the excitement was real. It had been the unanimous opinion of Kemp, Condella, Burbank, Pope, Old Adam, and the other senior members of the troupe that no traveling Shakespearean group had ever been invited to perform before the Archon before, We had no idea what to expect.

The dragoman who'd come to the church—if it was the same one, they all looked alike to me—was in the control cab of the sledge with various Archon cabiri and we were on the open freight pallet behind, where the human coffins were usually carried, so there was no chance for further conversation with the dragoman. The cabiri that the Archons had designed for the *Muse* and other old human spacecraft I'd seen—Shakespearean troupe, *perfecti*, and physiocrat—were more huge metal-spider than organic, but I noticed more patches of flesh and real hands and even a mouth, more lipped and human-looking than the dragoman's, on the cabiri in the sledge cab. The flesh, lips, teeth, fingers, and the rest looked as if they had come from a human-being parts bin. This was disturbing.

It was also disturbing to be in full costume and makeup so long *before* the performance. We carried along any changes in costume we'd need and a few props—chairs, a table, daggers, and the like—but no backdrops or scenery. And we assumed we'd have none of the computer-controlled lighting or microphone pickups that were always part of our performances at the *Muse* tents.

The sledge slid two meters above the rock road as it rose toward the keep of Mezel-Goull.

We'd never seen the spaceport or a funeral barge from up close before and we all stared as the sledge reached the cliff ledge and silently floated past the perfectly flat landing area. The barge was as grim as its purpose and huge, a three-siloed gray-black smooth-hulled mass that floated five meters above the scorch-blackened rock. Ramps led down to temperature-controlled storage sheds. More of the disturbing flesh-and-metal cabiri were loading human-sized sarcophagi up dark ramps.

The interior of the barge glowed dim red. The ship was large enough to carry tens and tens of thousands of sarcophagi.

There were three other Archon ships at the keep's spaceport. We'd seen such ships before, passing them during our transit from Kenoma to Pleroma or the reverse, but those were always video images, fast glimpses, and fuzzy, distant holos. The close-up reality of the three gray, grim, massive, heavily gunned and blistered and turreted, shaped and shielded vessels reminded all of us that the Archons were a fierce breed. After all these centuries we had no idea who or what their enemies were in the dark light-years beyond the Tell—we knew only that they were subservient to the Poimen, *Demiurgos*, and mythical Abraxi—but these ships were built to fight. They were, all of us were thinking in silence, destroyers of worlds.

The keep loomed larger than we had imagined. From the *Muse*, during our previous visits to the arbeiter town below, we'd guessed the height of the Archon castle to be about a thousand feet, its width about two-thirds that as its shape conformed to the narrow precipice a mile here above the black sulfur sea, but as we approached we realized that it must be more than two hundred stories tall. The gray-black stone was not stone but metal. Everywhere along its walls were blisters and bulges, much like on their warships, but here long rivulets and streaks of rust ran down. The streaks were the color of dried blood.

Some of the window slits far above glowed a dull orange.

"I need to take a piss," said our apprentice Pig. He started to climb down from the slowly moving sledge.

"Stay on," snapped Kemp.

"But..." began Pig.

"I need to go as well," said Kyder, costumed well as one of the three weird sisters in the first scene. "I doubt if they'll have lavatories in the Archon heap."

"*Stay on the goddamned sledge*," shouted Kemp. "If you get left behind, we won't be able to put on the show."

As if the dragoman or cabiri in the cab had heard him, the sledge began spinning and climbing higher then, swirling in the air to fifty feet of altitude, then a hundred, then three hundred. Everyone grabbed everyone, backed away from the open edge of the freight bed, and dropped to at least one knee.

The sledge swung out over the edge of the cliff. Acid breakers crashed onto fang-sharp boulders five thousand feet below us.

"Oh, fuck me!" cried the Pig. I could see the wet stain spreading down his brown tights and I also felt the sudden urge to urinate.

Six hundred feet up on the wall of stained metal-rock, high on the western side of the keep that hung out over the cliff's edge a mile above the sea, there came a great grinding and a trapezoid of light fifty or sixty feet high began to shape itself.

The sledge floated forward and we entered the keep.

THE SCOTTISH PLAY was difficult to do well under the best of conditions, and I would not say that the Archon keep of Mezel-Goull provided the best of conditions.

Our stage was a circular shelf about sixty feet across at the bottom of a giant well at the center of the keep. Or perhaps "well" isn't the proper word here, even though the lightning-roiled sky was visible through the round opening far above, since the rock-steel cliffs on all sides of our circle opened wider the higher they went. I estimated the walls here to be about three hundred feet high. All along the rough circle of stone were small cave openings, and outside these openings, on irregular slabs and ledges, sat the Archons—certainly more than a thousand of them. Perhaps two or three thousand.

Hanging by their filament hair around this almost gladiatorial space were dragomen—I guessed fifty, but there could have been more—attached to the crouching Archons' sensory nerve bundles only by their filaments. Each dragoman's synaptic fibers connected to at least twenty or thirty Archons, who looked more insectoid than ever here in their native habitat, crouched and multilegged on their rock shelves, some holding their red nerve bundle packets away from their bodies with a pair of hands, looking much like an ancient holo I once saw on Earth of a bearded Jesus Christ (or perhaps it was Mohammed; one of the ancient gods at least) holding forth his red heart as if only recently ripped from his chest.

The only bright light was on our solid circle of yellow stone or metal. All the rest of the rising cavernous space was lighted by the dimmest of red glows from the cavern openings. Lightning continued to ripple and tear above us, but something muffled all sound from beyond the keep.

Our performance was perhaps the best we'd ever given.

Kemp and Condella played the Thane and his Queen, of course, with Burbank outdoing himself as the drunken Porter. Watching Condella as Lady Ma...as the Queen... reminded me of why she was one of the most incredible touring actresses in the Tell.

For years I had played Macduff's son but more recently had been upgraded to Lennox, one of the Scottish thanes, so I got to be onstage between the three witches' scenes during the second scene where King Duncan, Malcolm, and the rest of us spy "the bloody man," and I confess that my first line—"What a haste looks through his eyes! So should he look that seems to speak things strange"—came out as more powerful squeak than bold pronouncement.

This unique setting for our performance did not seem to distract the others. Kemp was extraordinary. Condella transcended herself, although—as she once told me bitterly—"The Queen in this damned Scottish Play is just *too* good a role, Master Wilbr. Every time she's onstage everyone else, even the Thane, is thrown into shadow. Shakespeare had to keep her offstage, the same as he had to kill Mercutio early in *Romeo and Juliet* or let him take over the play, like a callower Hamlet wandering loose." And it was true, I noticed back then, that Lady Ma...the Queen...exits in act 3, scene 4, and isn't seen again until she returns, already lost to madness, at the start of act 5.

Aglaé, the most beautiful young actress on this world or any other world, the most beautiful actress in the Tell or beyond, played one of the three Weird Sisters and her makeup was almost, not quite, good enough to hide her beauty behind warts, wrinkles, a fake nose, and a wispy beard.

As I exited...which meant just to walk outside the circle of light onto the dark part of the round slab of floor...Aglaé came on and cried, "'Where hast thou been, sister?'"

Anne, as the second witch, answered, "'Killing swine.'"

Standing in the offstage darkness, I peered up at the ungainly slabs and ledges and cavemouths. Did these alien things know what witches were? What swine were? Presumably the latter since they had chosen pigs as one of the few forms of livestock to bring along with their human slaves.

The third witch cried as if blind, "'Sister, where thou?'"

Aglaé responded, voice husky and ancient, "'A sailor's wife had chestnuts in her lap. And munched and munched and munched. "Give me" quoth I. "Aroint thee, witch," the rump-fed runnion cries. Her husband's to Aleppo gone, master o' th' *Tiger*. But in a sieve I'll thither sail, and, like a rat without a tail, I'll do, I'll do, and I'll do.'"

Dear Abraxas above, I thought, my heart pounding wildly, *these Archons will not understand a word or thought of this. What help can the soulless dragomen be? They see and hear and maybe translate the words, but how can you translate Shakespeare to alien minds?*

And hard on the heels of that thought came a more terrible certainty: *this is some sort of trial; the Archons are deciding whether to let us live or not.*

WE PLAYED ON. Sans props, sans scenery, sans curtain, sans human audience.

When one act ended, we would all pause outside the circle of light for a few seconds and then begin the next. Kemp later told me that this was more or less the way Shakespeare and his people had done it in their day; that acts and scenes, as separate entities, were a later invention.

One of Kemp's earliest lines, to the witches, was "The Thane of Cawdor lives. Why do you dress me in borrowed clothes."

Dear God, I loved such phrases. "The Thane of Cawdor." It evoked human ages and vital human barbarity long lost to all of us. But what could it possibly mean to the hooded, earless, handless, eyeless, faceless Archons on their bug ledges above?

By the time Kemp choked out these anguished lines, I was sure that we'd already signed our own death warrants through our very incomprehensibility to this chitinous audience:

> If it were done when 'tis done, then 'twere well
> It were done quickly. If th' assassination
> Could trammel up the consequence and catch
> With his surcease success, that but this blow
> Might be the be-all and the end-all here,
> But here, upon this bank and shoal of time,
> We'd jump the life to come...

When suddenly, from the dark ledges above there came a susurration as of many insect breaths blowing over violin-bow forelimbs, followed by a growing *chrr... chrrr...chrrrr...chrrrrr.*

Kemp as the Thane did not miss a beat, but offstage in the dark I leaned on Tooley, one of the soldiers, as I stared up into the dark, straining almost painfully to see. Coeke leaned over and whispered fiercely, "I didn't know the Archons had wings, did you?"

There was more *chrrrring* during the next hour, the loudest—it drowned out the ensuing dialogue and made even our most unperturbable players pause a second—came, for no reason we will ever understand, after Burbank as the Porter gave his "equivocation" speech:

Marry, sir, nose-painting, sleep, and urine. Lechery, sir, it provokes, and unprovokes: it provokes the desire, but it takes away the performance. Therefore much drink may be said to be an equivocator with lechery. It makes him, and it mars him; it sets him on and it takes him off; it persuades him and disheartens him; makes him stand to and not stand to; in conclusion, equivocates him in a sleep, and giving him the lie, leaves him.

The *chrrrring* went on and on for almost three minutes. The drone-hum of wings was so loud I expected to look up to see the Archons flitting about this hive-tunnel space like so many hornets.

Why? What could they possibly know of drunkenness or desire, lechery or impotence? Much less the effect alcohol has on men before, during, or after the sex act?

I looked at Aglaé, still in her witch makeup and costume. As if reading my mind, she shook her head.

In no time, in an eternity, it was over.

Malcolm—Gough—the new King of Scotland, had his final words while Macduff stood there holding a fair likeness of Kemp's head by the hair. It reminded me of the dangling dragomen above.

"'That calls upon us, by the grace of grace,'" boomed Gough-Malcolm, "'we will perform in measure, time, and place. So thanks to all at once, and to each one, whom we invite to see us crowned at Scone.'"

Those onstage bowed.

The dead rose and bowed.

Those of us in the darkened wings came into the circle of light and bowed.

Nothing.

No applause. Not a cough. Not even a *chrrring* of wings. Silence.

After a moment of this excruciating nothing, the light in and on our circle went out. We could see that the ledges and slabs above were empty. Even the hanging dragomen were gone.

A trapezoid opened in a solid wall behind us. The gravity sledge floated in.

Kemp, still in makeup, refused to board—or allow us to board—until the dragoman standing by the cab gave us some indication of what the Archons had thought.

The dragoman—I thought it was the same one that had come to the church that morning, but was not sure—said, "You are no longer the Earth's Men."

Kemp opened his mouth but decided not to speak.

"From this moment forward, you are the Heresiarch's Men," said the dragoman.

WE RENDEZVOUSED IN orbit with the Archon warship exactly as instructed. This was to be the first time we ever penetrated the Pleroma following anything but a funeral barge. As far as we knew, it was the first time that any human ship—player troupe, *perfecti*, or physiocrat—had ever entered the Abyss behind anything but a funeral barge.

It was also the first time that anyone other than a member of the troupe had traveled with us in the *Muse*.

I still thought the dragoman was the same one who'd come to the church and driven us to the keep, but I'd seen enough of them in the cone of Mezel-Goull to know they actually all looked alike.

Once we were safely in the Pleroma, surrounded by that objective golden glow, the dragoman had an odd request. He wanted to see the *Muse*. Herself.

Kemp and Condella and Burbank and a few of the co-owners had to confer about that. We had never let an outsider see the true Muse. Except for when we were children trying to frighten each other, we seldom went down there ourselves.

In the end, they relented. What choice did they have? Kemp did ask the dragoman—"Are you still in touch with the Archon? Even though your...ah...hair...isn't connected? Even here in the Abyss?"

The lipless large-eyed man-thing stared in a way that I almost could have interpreted as amusement. "We are always united in the flame of Abraxas," he/it said.

It was from the Fourth Sermon to the Dead.

Good and evil are united in the flame.
Good and evil are united in the growth of the tree.
Life and love oppose each other in their own divinity.

What the hell. They decided to let the dragoman visit the *Muse*.

For some reason, Kemp beckoned me to join the four of them showing the dragoman the way.

The body of the *Muse* slept through eternity in a small compartment past the sleeping level where our bunks lay empty, below the circular common room where a few of the others looked up at us with unanswered questions in their eyes as we passed, beneath the throbbing engine room where Tooley used to let me look in through the thick blue glass at the star-flame of our fusion ship's heart when I was a boy, down a ladder and through two hatches into a space barely large enough for the five of us humans and the dragoman to stand in a circle around the fluid-filled sphere in the center.

She floated there in the thick, blue liquid. Long dead but not dead. Her body mummified. Her eyes long since turned to cobwebs. Her breasts now flattened to wrinkled mummy's dugs. Her sex lost. Her once-red hair mostly gone, the wispy remnants floating like a baby chick's fuzz. Her lips stretched back to reveal all her skull-teeth. Her arms were folded in front of her as she floated, look-ing as fleshless and fragile as broken bird's wings, her thumbs folded in flat against her fluid-shriveled palms.

"Who was she?" asked the dragoman.

"No one knows," said Condella. "Some say she was named Sophia."

"She wouldn't answer if you asked her through the ship?" the dragoman asked.

"She wouldn't understand the question," said Kemp.

"I could ask her directly," said the dragoman. The thought of that made my skin go cold.

The *Muse* spoke then, her voice coming from the walls. I don't know if any of the others jumped, but I did. "We have exited the Abyss and returned to the Kenoma. This system is not numbered. These worlds are unnamed. We are no longer in the Archon warship's pleromic wake. Another craft has taken control and ordered me to follow it until further notice. All imaging surfaces are now active."

"Another craft?" I said, looking from Kemp to Burbank to the dragoman.

The dragoman was clutching his head so fiercely that his ten spatulate fingers compressed white. "They're gone," he gasped.

"Who's gone?" asked Kemp.

"The Archons. For the first time...in my...existence. There is...no...contact." The dragoman fell to the deck and wrapped his long arms around his legs as he curled into a tight and rocking fetal position.

"Whose ship is it then?" asked Condella.

Black fluid ran from the dragonman's eyes and open mouth as he gasped. "The Poimen."

In the globe of blue liquid, the mummy of the *Muse* writhed, extended her withered arms, and opened her empty eyes.

WE GATHERED IN the common room. Tooley and Pig laid the unconscious dragoman on an old acceleration couch; we could not tell if he was still alive. Black fluid continued to seep from his mouth, ears, eyes, and unseen orifices under his genital flap and none of the rest of us wished to touch him.

Tooley wiped his hands and hurried to unroll view-strips along the curved outer bulkhead. Within minutes it felt as if we were on a high platform open to three-dimensional space in all directions.

Kemp came down from above. "The *Muse* is not answering questions or responding to navigation requests," he said. "We're not even under power. As far as we can tell, there's no pleromic wake, but we're still under the influence of that ship pulling us toward the gas giant."

The Muse *not answering questions or responding to orders?* We all stared at one another with terror in our eyes. This had never happened. It *couldn't* happen. If the *Muse* failed, malfunctioned, died, we were all dead. I remembered the flailing and stretching and silent gape-mouthed screams of her mummy in the blue sphere below and wondered if somehow we had all killed her by following the Archon warship through the Pleroma.

I realized that the fusion thum and slight additional weight of in-system thrust was absent for the first time ever in our nonpleromic travels. The only thing keep-ing us from floating around the room was the sternward pressure of the internal tension fields. At least that meant that some power was still being generated.

Watching the scene through the huge viewstrip windows did nothing to quell our terror.

We were hurtling toward a gas-giant world with a velocity the *Muse* would never have allowed or been able to obtain. Ahead of us was a bluish-gray ship, size impossible to determine without references or radar that the *Muse* would not or could not bring online even after repeated requests. The blue-gray ship seemed solid yet was impossibly malleable, shifting shapes constantly: now an aerodynamic dart, almost winged; now a blue spheroid; now a muscular mass of curves and bubbles that made the missing Archon warship look as crudely made as an iron boomerang.

Then all of us ceased looking at the ship towing us and stared slack-jawed at the approaching world.

Worlds, I should say, because the green and blue and white gas giant—there was no doubt it was a Jovian-sized world—was accompanied by a dozen or more hurtling moons and a ring.

I'd seen hundreds of gas giants in my travels from Pleroma to the Archon worlds of the Tell, Jupiter and Saturn being only the first and those only briefly glimpsed, but never had I seen a world like this. None of us had.

Instead of the red, orange, yellow, and turquoise methane stripes common to most such giants, this world alternated bands of blue and white. Massive cloud-storms that must have been as large as Jupiter's Red Spot swirled in cyclonic splendor, but these were white storms—Earth-like hurricanes—and they traveled along blue bands that suggested oceans of water thousands of miles below.

This alone would have made us gawk—an Earth-like gas-giant world of such beauty—not to mention the dozen, no fifteen at least, no, now seventeen moons we could see hurtling above the multihued equatorial rings that girdled the big planet some tens of thousands of miles above its shimmering atmosphere, but it was the signs of civilization that kept our mouths open and our eyes wide.

To say the world was obviously inhabited would have been the understatement of all time.

The gas giant was about two-thirds illuminated by its yellow sun, but the dark slice beyond the curve of terminator was as brilliantly lighted as the glaring blue and white daytime side. Straight and winding strings of lights by the millions showed linear communities or highways or flyways or coastlines or spaceports or...we did not know what. Constellations of lights, by the billions it seemed, showed cities or, because the constellations were moving, perhaps just the denizens themselves, radiant as gods.

Buildings...towers...crystalline structures rose out of the clouds and then out of the atmosphere itself; not one or a few, but hundreds of them. They moved with the revolution of the planet. Several rose not only through the atmosphere but up through the orbital rings around the giant world...rings which we now could see were made up of artificial moonlets or structures by the million. The myriad of sparkling orbital objects looked if they were going to crash into the tallest crystal towers with the speed of meteors, of comets, but at the last minute the streams of particles—each object hundreds of times larger than the *Muse*, we realized—parted like a river current around a rock.

The space between the big planet and the moons was filled not only with the countless objects that made up equatorial rings, and with the fluid-filled cords to the moons, but with more millions of rising and descending flecks catching sunlight and throwing off their own flames. Spacecraft, we presumed, rising and descending from the world.

"Dear Abraxas," whispered Burbank. "How tall are those structures?"

We could see the towers' shadows now, thrown across entire continents below them, across seas of clouds. The base of each tower was invisible beneath the white and blue—perhaps the fluid-filled towers passed through the entire giant world like so many crystalline stakes driven through the planet's heart—but their summits and upper floors rose deep into the vacuum of cislunar space.

"Hundreds of miles high, at least," said Heminges who knew a few technical things. "Thousands, I think."

"That's impossible," said Condella.

The towing ship slowed and we slowed with it as we entered the cislunar system.

"Look at this," said Tooley, who had pushed some of the viewstrips to their maximum magnification.

From farther out we'd seen the writhing strands rising from the world toward the many moons, but now we could see that not only were they continuous—connected all the way from the giant planet to the many hurtling moons, some of which must have been the size of Earth or 25–25–261B, but the cords, each anchored somewhere on the big planet, were transparent and hollow.

"Those must each be three or four hundred miles in diameter," whispered Gough.

"Impossible," said Kemp.

Coeke nodded and rubbed stubble on his massive jaw. "It is impossible, but look…" He stabbed a blunt, black finger into the holo of the viewstrip. "There's something moving inside each connecting thread."

"Are those things bridges?" asked Alleyn in hushed tones.

"More like umbilicals, I think," said Hywo. "Conduits. They're filled with liquid. Things are…swimming… moving both directions in that fluid."

"Not possible," Kemp said.

"We're closing on that tallest tower pretty fast," said Philp.

He was right. Kemp, Tooley, and Burbank, our three most common interlocutors with the *Muse*, began calling to her with some alarm in their voices—if we needed to fire engines to brake, she needed to do it *now*—but the *Muse* did not answer.

"Oh, Abraxas, embracer of all opposites, terror of the sun, heart of the sun, help us," prayed Old Adam.

A blue sphere about twelve feet across floated through the hull. We clambered and leaped to get out of its way.

At first, in my fear and confusion, I thought it was the blue-fluid-filled globe below that held the mummy of the *Muse*, but this was larger and something else. The blue was a different color and the sphere glowed from within. There was a living being in the water or fluid; the creature was golden, vaguely amphibian, and about eight feet long. I could see a face of sorts, eyes of sorts, a slash of a mouth or feeding orifice, large gills, gold and green scales, and two vestigial arms, like those of a malformed fetus, with lovely small hands.

Suddenly the still corpse of the dragoman spoke. "We are sorry we injured this member of your species. He is no longer living. We shall resurrect him to make amends."

None of us spoke until Aglaé managed, "Are you the Poimen?"

"We did not mean to damage this unit while we were taking your ship from the possession of the petty rulers," said the dead dragoman, a black fluid as viscous as ink still running from the corners of his mouth and eyes as he lay there on the couch.

I remembered my catechism, Father teaching me in the glass room through the endless rainy afternoons on Earth. Centuries ago, after our first contact with the Archons and the end of our species' rule of self, Abraxas had revealed four levels of our masters, four stages of our own eternal evolution should our physical bodies be returned to Earth and our *psyche* and *pneuma* be pure enough to ascend the four circles.

The Archons were the petty rulers. The Poimen, whom no humans in our lifetimes had ever glimpsed, were the shepherds. The *Demiurgos* were the half-makers. (It was they who had created our faulty, failed Earth and universe.) The Abraxi were the shattered vessels of Abraxas, the ultimate God of Opposites.

The dragoman sat up on his couch, set his splayed feet on the deck, and wiped ink from his lipless mouth. His synaptic filaments hung down like wet vines. His black-rimmed eyes stared at us with no obvious signs of alarm. "What happened while I was dead?"

Before we could answer, he spoke again, but his voice had that somehow flatter, infinitely more vacant tone it had held a moment before when the Poimen amphibian in the blue globe had spoken through him.

"We will be docking within moments. You will choose one of your *mimesis* episodes for performance in one hour and eleven minutes. An appropriate place will be made ready for you. There will be those there to receive your images and sounds...an audience."

"One hour and eleven minutes!" shouted Kemp. None of us had slept for at least thirty-six hours. We'd already performed *Much Ado About Nothing* and the most successful performance of *The Tragedy of Macbe...* the Scottish Play...that we had ever seen, much less participated in.

"One hour and eleven minutes?" he cried again.

But the Poimen and its sphere were gone, floated back through the hull and out of sight.

THE POIMEN SHIP placed the *Muse of Fire* gently in a niche near the top of the crystal tower—we passed through some sort of tough but permeable membrane that held the liquid inside, not to mention its inhabitants, safe and separate from the cold of space—and then other gold and green and reddish and blue-gilled forms piloting small machines, open and delicate jet sledges which they guided with their tiny hands, took us down the thousand miles or two of flooded crystal column at an impossible speed.

"Supercavitation," muttered Tooley.

"What?" snapped Kemp.

"Nothing."

Our one engineer seemed sullen since the *Muse* quit speaking to him.

We spent most of the hour and ten minutes during the descent—the water-scooter Poimen pulled and pushed us through clouds and what seemed like blue and turquoise seas—arguing about what to perform.

"*Romeo and Juliet*," argued Alleyn and Aglaé. Of course they would argue for that play. It was theirs. Kemp and Condella and Adam and even Heminges were old farts and demoted to secondary and tertiary roles in that play.

Kemp vetoed the idea. "This may be the most important performance we ever do," said the troupe leader. "We have to put on the *best*—the best of the Bard, the best of ourselves."

"You said that yesterday," Alleyn said dryly. "For the Archons."

"Well, it was true then," said Kemp. He was so exhausted that his voice was raw. "It's truer now."

"What then?" asked Burbank. "*Hamlet*? *Lear*?"

"*Lear*," decided Kemp.

What a surprise! I thought bitterly. Kemp decides on the play tailored to Kemp on our most important performance ever. The universe ages, Earth loses its oceans, the human race is subjugated and turned into cultureless futureless slaves, but actors still count lines.

"Will I be Cordelia?" asked Aglaé.

Of course she would. She'd been Cordelia in the past twenty performances, with Condella as the infinitely rancid older Goneril.

"No, I will be Cordelia," announced Condella in tones that brooked no opposition. "You will be Regan. Becca can be Goneril."

"But," began Aglaé, obviously crushed, "how can you play..." She stopped. How can an actress tell another actress that she's decades too old for a part, even when it would be obvious to the most groundling groundling?

Kemp said, "These are *aliens*. We've never seen these...Poimen...and they've never seen us. They can't tell our ages. They almost certainly can't tell our genders. I'm not sure they can tell our *species*."

"Then how in the hell can they get anything out of the play?" snapped Heminges.

I thought he had something there. But then again, I remembered, the Poimen *were* gods...of a sort.

The ship had been lowered to some appropriate depth, although shafts of sunlight still filtered down through the clear blue waters. It was as if we were in a blue and gold cathedral. Hundreds of the Poimen, who weren't men at all despite that part of their name (or the name Abraxas had given them), swam and shuttled around us, some being pulled by their jet-sled craft, some using other means of propulsion, some inside larger craft and looking out through transparent hulls. The depths were also filled with larger submersibles of varied design, some moving in obvious lanes but others shimmering like gigantic schools of metal fish. Far below us, the waters grew darker and larger things, living things I thought, moved with leviathan slowness.

Kemp gave the assignments. I hoped for Edmund, of course, all of us younger actors did, if we couldn't get

Edgar, but received the part of Albany's servant. At least I got to kill and die onstage. (I confess I've never understood that servant's motivation.)

Heminges was to be Edmund, the bastard in every sense. I think I might have cast him as Edgar; Heminges is crazy enough out of character to play Tom o'Bedlam half the time. But Alleyn got Edgar. Pope was the Duke of Cornwall, evil Regan's stupid husband—I could see Pope squinting dubiously at Aglaé (he'd never had such a young Regan). Gough got the good role of the Earl of Kent.

There was a tradition in Shakespeare's day for Lear's Fool, a sort of holy fool, to be played by the same actor who plays Cordelia—the Fool is never onstage when Cordelia is and he disappears completely when her major scenes begin— but this wasn't going to work with tonight's casting.

I would have given my left testicle to play the Fool, but Burbank got it.

Adam got the Old Man—what else?—and Philp was the courtly, brave, and courting Duke of Burgundy. Coeke was to be Curan, Gloucester's retainer, and Hywo Gloucester.

The lesser roles, gentlemen, servants, soldiers, and messengers, were quickly parceled out. We knew all the parts—or were supposed to.

Pyk came up and tried to get Kemp's attention, but our Fearless Leader was too busy making costume choices and discussing staging—Christ, we hated theater-in-the-round and prayed to Abraxas that this place would not be like Mezel-Goull.

"What is it, Pig?" I whispered.

"The *Muse*," he whispered wetly in my ear.

"What about her?"

"You'd better come see, Wilbr."

I followed him down through the engine room, through the double hatches, down the ladder to the tiny room holding the *Muse*'s sphere and mummy. I admit that I was a little nervous being in there just with Pig after watching the *Muse*'s gyrations and eyes opening an hour or so earlier.

Her eyes were still opened, but no longer empty. They were complete and blue and looking at me. No mummy now. The naked young woman floating in the blue fluid was more beautiful and younger than Aglaé. Her restored red hair floated around her like a fiery nimbus.

She did not quite smile at me but her gaze registered my presence.

I said to Pig, "Jesus Christ and Abraxas's rooster's balls. Let's get the hell out of here." And we did. But what I'd actually thought of in those seconds I stared into the resurrected *Muse*'s eyes was an old catechism line from Saint Jung: "The dream is like a woman. It will have the last word as it had the first."

SAYING IT WAS an extraordinary performance of *King Lear* would not be praise enough. It was beyond extraordinary. It would have won the laurel wreath at any gathering of the Bard Troupes on Stratford 111 at any time in the last twelve hundred years or more. The legendary Barbassesserra could not have created a better Lear that night than Kemp did. His very exhaustion lent more credence to the king's age, despair, and madness. And I have to admit that Condella was tragically radiant and perfectly, absurdly stubborn as Cordelia. After a few minutes, I forgot her age—so I had to assume the Poimen never noticed.

The Poimen.

They allowed us to extend and light our own stage from the *Muse*. The ship had recovered sufficiently to handle the stage and basic lighting, although the cabiri were not functional. We were able to use our dressing rooms and regular arras and stage exits. But we did not need a tent where we performed.

Our ship and stage were on a sort of shell within a bubble. I have no idea what energies kept the bubble intact, our air recycled, or the pressures of the alien ocean from rushing in. But the bubble was invisible and it did not distort vision in or out as glass or plastic would. We did not float around or bob; the stage felt as firm beneath us as it had the night before at Mezel-Goull, but this was obviously an illusion since some moments into the performance we realized that our stage and ship and bubble were rotating three hundred and sixty degrees, even turning as they rotated. At times we were completely upside down—the surface of the ocean invisible beneath our feet and stage and stern of the *Muse*—but somehow the stage was always *down*. Our inner ear did not register the changes and gravity did not vary. (In fact, the gravity itself was suspicious, since it felt one-Earth average on such a gigantic planet.) But the turning and rotation were very slow, so if one did not look out beyond the proscenium for any length of time, there was no vertigo involved. When I did look, it took my breath away.

The water—if it was water—was incredibly clear. I could see scores of the huge blue and green crystal towers, each lighted from within, each with a central twin shaft filled with rising and falling liquids and passengers, each rising into sunlight and atmosphere above—where countless more of the Poimen floated and flitted—and then into space above that, each also extending down to the purple depths miles beneath us.

The Poimen floated around us by the thousands or by the tens of thousands. Without staring I couldn't tell, and one can't stare at the audience during a performance, even when the fear of vertigo *isn't* a factor. I could see that they were not all the same. Shafts of sunlight columning down from the rough seas above illuminated a bewildering variety of Poimen sizes, shapes, and iridescent colors. Some of the creatures were as large as Archon spacecraft; others as small as the koi in funeral ponds on Earth. All showed the same sort of flat face, black eyes, throbbing gills, and tiny arms, at least relative to their body size, and delicate hands as our first visitor in the sphere that had come through the *Muse*'s hull.

Kemp and Burbank had gone on about how they hated performing in theater-in-the-round as at Mezel-Goull, but here we were in a theater of three dimensions, with audience above, to the side, and partially beneath us, thousands of pairs of eyes focused on us from all directions, and all of them moving in our constantly rotating field of vision. A lesser troupe would have had trouble going on. We weren't a lesser troupe.

Did the Poimen understand us? Did they get the slightest hint of what our "mimesis episode" was about? Could these sea-space creatures understand the foggiest outline of the themes and depths of Shakespeare's tale of age and loss and ultimate devastation, much less follow the beautiful and archaic song of our language?

I had no idea. I'm sure Kemp and Burbank and Condella and the others carrying the burden of the performance had no idea. We carried on.

Burbank once told me that his father—who had led the Earth's Men longer than any other person and who was almost certainly the finest actor ever to come out of our troupe—had said to him that *King Lear* precluded and baffled all commentary because the experience of it was beyond theater, beyond even the literature and art and music we had when humans had literature and art and music. *King Lear* and *Hamlet,* the older Burbank had told his son, went even beyond the false but beautiful holy scriptures humans used to have before the Archons and their superiors showed us the truth. The Torah, the Talmud, the New Testament, the Koran, the Upanishads, the RigVeda, the Agama, the Mahavastu, the Adi Granth, the Sutta Pitaka, the Dasabhumisvara, the Mahabharata, and the Bible, to name only a few, were false but beautiful, and important for evolving human hearts and minds, said the elder Burbank, but all receded before the unfathomable truths of *Hamlet* and *King Lear.* And where *Hamlet* explored the infinite bounds of consciousness, *Lear* delved the absolute depths of mortality, hopelessness, communication failed, trust betrayed, and the threads of chaos which weave our fates.

I think those are some of the words and phrases Burbank told me his father used. One does get in the habit of memorizing very quickly when traveling with actors.

They'd only been words to me until this night— pleasant theatrical hyperbole (which is redundant, Philp would argue, since all theater, however nuanced, is mimetic hyperbole of life)—but this day, this night, *this* performance of *King Lear* made me understand what Burbank's father had been trying to say.

When Kemp, as Lear gone mad and wearing his crown of weeds and flowers, said to Hywo as the blinded Gloucester

> *If thou wilt weep my fortunes, take my eyes.*
> *I know thee well enough; thy name is Gloucester.*
> *Thou must be patient. We came crying hither;*
> *Thou know'st the first time that we smell the air*
> *We wawl and cry. I will preach to thee. Mark.*

and then Kemp slowly took off his crown not of thorns but of faded flowers and tangled dry grasses and Hywo/ Gloucester wept

> *Alack, alack, the day!*

only to have mad Kemp/Lear pat his back and console him with absolute hopelessness—

> *When we are born, we cry that we are come*
> *To this great stage of fools.*

I wept.

I'm glad I was offstage and behind the arras, away from those thousands of staring fish-eyes, because I wept like the child I don't remember actually being.

By the time Lear carried his dead daughter onstage and pronounced those five heaviest words in the history of the theater—"Never, never, never, never, never."—I could no longer stand. I had to sit down to sob.

And then the play was over.

There was no applause, no noise, no movement, no visible reaction at all from the schools and congregations and aggregations and flocks of Poimen in the blue beyond our bubble.

Kemp and the others bowed. We all took our curtain call.

The Poimen moved away in the sea currents and submersibles.

We stood there, exhausted, looking into the wings at the players who hadn't played but who seemed equally exhausted, and then, almost in unison, we looked at the dragoman where he sat listlessly in the wings, elbows on his knees, eyes unblinking and seemingly unfocused.

"Well?" demanded Kemp, his voice almost gone and as old-sounding as the dying Lear's. "Did they like it? Did they *hear* it?"

"Why do you ask me?" said the dragoman in his flat squeak.

"Weren't they in *touch* with you?" bellowed Burbank.

"How do I know?" said the dragoman. "Were they in touch with *you*?"

Kemp advanced on the spindly dragoman as though he were going to pummel him, but just then our bubble went dim as surely as if someone had put a towel over a bird's cage.

The dragoman jerked to his feet, not to meet Kemp's charge—he was not even looking at Kemp—and said in a different tone, "You have one hour and eleven minutes to rest. And then you and your ship shall be transported elsewhere."

Our view out the bubble had disappeared with the light. There was no sense of whether we were being moved or not, but we knew from the motion during the performance that something was dampening our sense of inertia in this cage. We went back into the *Muse*.

NONE OF US slept during those seventy-one minutes. Some collapsed on their bunks or just stood in showers letting the hot water run over them—all of the *Muse*'s systems were functioning now—but about half the troupe met in the larger of the two common rooms on the upper deck.

"What's going on?" demanded Pig.

I thought our youngest apprentice had summed up the essential question pretty well with those three words.

"They're testing us," said Aglaé. She'd been a brilliant Regan.

"Testing us?" demanded Kemp. He and Burbank and Condella and the senior members of the troupe were glaring at her.

"What else could it be?" asked my weary and oh-so-lovely Aglaé. "No one's ever heard of a traveling troupe being forced to perform before the Archons before, much less before these...*Poimen*...if they *are* actually Poimen. We're being tested."

"For what?" asked Heminges. "And why us? And what happens if we fail?" He should have been as exhausted as Kemp or Burbank or Condella—he'd had important roles in all three of the performances we'd done in the last forty-eight hours—but fatigue just made his face look more handsomely gaunt and alert and Iago-cunning.

No one had an answer, not even Aglaé. But I began to think that she was right—we were being put to the test—but I could think of no reason, after all these centuries, that a traveling troupe, or the human race for that matter, should be tested. Hadn't we been tested and found wanting those first years when the Archon, on the order of *their* masters we were made to understand, ended our freedom and cultures and politics and sense of history and dreams of ever going to the stars on our own? What more could they take from us if we failed their goddamned tests?

It made me want to weep, but I'd already blubbered like a baby enough luring that extraordinary, never-to-be-repeated performance of *King Lear*, so I went up to the topside observation room to talk to Tooley for a few minutes, and then, when the birdcage towel was lifted and the *Muse* informed us that we were in the Pleroma again in the wake of the Poimen ship, I climbed down through all the decks to the tiny room where the newly resurrected *Muse* floated in her clear blue nutrient.

I FELT LIKE a voyeur.

In my previous eleven years aboard the *Muse*, I'd rarely come down here to her tiny compartment. There was no real reason to—the *Muse* spoke to us through the ship, *was* the ship, and we were no closer to her down here near the mummified husk she'd left behind so many centuries ago than anywhere else on the ship: less close here really, since she seemed alive elsewhere. But more than that, I was scared to come here as a boy. Philp and I used to dare each other to go down in the dark place to see the dead lady. I rarely came down here as a man.

But now I had, and I felt like a voyeur.

What had been a brown, wrinkled, eyeless mummy was now a beautiful young woman, perhaps Aglaé's age, perhaps even younger, but—I had to admit—even more beautiful. Her red hair was so dark it looked almost black in the blue fluid. Her open eyes—I did not see her blink but at times her eyes were suddenly closed for long periods—were blue. Her skin was almost pure white, lighter than anyone else's aboard. Her nipples were pink. Her lips were a darker pink. The perfect V of her pubic hair was red and curly and dense.

I looked away, thought about going back up to my bunk.

"It's all right," said a soft voice behind me. "She does not mind if you look."

I just about jumped straight up through the hatch eight feet above me.

The dragoman stood there. His fibroneural filaments hung limp on his pale shoulders. There were still black streaks and stains near the corners of his eyes and mouth.

"You're in touch with her?" I whispered.

"No, she's in touch with me."

"What is she saying?"

"Nothing."

"What happened to her?"

The dragoman said nothing. He seemed to be looking at an empty space between me and the blue sphere.

"Who restored her?" I asked, my voice echoing now in the tiny metal room. "The Poimen?"

"No."

"The *Archons*?" It did not seem possible.

"No."

"What does she want?"

The dragoman turned his lipless face toward me. "She tells you that the two of you should come here when it is your turn. Before you act."

"Two of us?" I repeated stupidly. "Which two? Act on what? Why does the *Muse* want me to come here?"

At that moment the ship shook and I felt the familiar ending of the buzz and tingle one feels when transiting the Pleroma, a sort of vibration of the bones and rising of the short hairs on the arm, and then came the slight but perceptible downward shift-shock I'd felt so many times when we transitioned back to the Kenoma of empty forms. Our universe.

"Jesus Christ Abraxas!" came Kemp's voice crashing over the intercom. "Everyone come up to the main common room. *Now!*"

TOOLEY, PIG, KEMP, and the others had run viewstrips from deck to ceiling around the large common room, and then added more strips across the ceilings. The *Muse*'s external imagers provided and integrated the views. It was as if this deck of the ship were open to space.

There was no Poimen ship ahead of us. We had been flung out of the Pleroma into this system like a stone from a catapult such as the ones we'd seen arbeiters on 30–08–16B9 use to move boulders miles up the mountains to build the Archon's keep.

We were hurtling toward a series of concentric translucent spheres surrounding a blinding blue-white star.

Each sphere was larger than the last, of course, but shafts of brilliant sunlight passed through each sphere to the next and then through the last one out to us. The *Muse* put up deep radar and other readings showing that there were more than a dozen spheres, each one mottled with dark continents and painted with blue seas.

"Eyes of Abraxas!" breathed Heminges. "This is not possible."

"It's not possible in a thousand ways," said Tooley. "According to *Muse*'s data there, we're one hundred and forty-four AU out from this star. There shouldn't be this much light reaching us...or this first, last, sphere. Unless each sphere were somehow refracting and refocusing the light...or magnifying it...or adding to it..."

We all stared at Tooley. Usually he spoke only to explain how he was unplugging toilets or greasing gears or some such. This was by far the longest speech any of us had ever heard from him.

I remembered that an AU was an astronomical unit, the distance Earth was from its sun. Most of the Archon worlds we visited lurked at around one AU from their suns.

144 AU out?

"There are a dozen spheres around this sun," came the *Muse*'s strangely young voice. "There are two separate but intersecting spheres at one AU, one at two AU, then others at three AU, five AU, eight AU, thirteen AU, twenty-one AU, thirty-four AU, fifty-five AU, eighty-nine AU, and this outer one at one hundred forty-four AU from the star."

"Fibonacci sequence," muttered Tooley.

"Precisely," said the *Muse*. "But it seems oddly inelegant. A series of orbiting Apollonian circles would have put more spheres of varying diameter within a closer radius to this star without the need for—"

"*Muse!*" interrupted Kemp. "We're approaching this outer sphere pretty damned quickly. Shouldn't you be firing the engines to slow us?"

"It would not help," said the *Muse*. "Our velocity upon leaving the Pleroma was a significant fraction of C, the speed of light. We have never entered any system from any pleromic wake at anything near this velocity. I do not even understand how we can maintain our integrity at this speed since the collision of isolated hydrogen particles alone should—"

"You mean you can't slow us?" interrupted Condella.

"Oh, yes, I can," said the *Muse*. "At my full thrust of four hundred gravities, it would take me a little over eight months to bring our velocity down. But we will impact the outer sphere in four minutes and fifteen seconds. Also, the ship's internal fields protect passengers...you...only up to thirty-one gravities. You would be, as the old saying goes, raspberry jam."

"Can you *miss* the outer sphere?" asked Aglaé. "Steer around it?"

The Muse only laughed. I had never heard her laugh before and I'm sure it not even the oldest members of the troupe had either.

No one said anything for a while.

Finally, Burbank ordered, "Show clock. Analog. Countdown."

A holographic clock appeared above a viewstrip, showing three minutes and twenty-two seconds until impact. The sweep hand continued moving backward toward zero.

Burbank wheeled on the dragoman who had been silent, great lidless eyes downcast, standing away from the rest of us who were almost forming a circle while staring at the clock and viewstrips. "Do you have any goddamned ideas?" barked Burbank. His tone sounded accusatorial, as if the dragoman had brought us to this end.

It turns out that someone with no lips can still smile. "Pray?" he said softly.

WHAT WOULD YOU do with three minutes left to live? I didn't pray. I didn't do anything else either, other than to look at Aglaé for a minute with more regret than I thought it possible for a person to hold. I was sorry that she and I would never make love. More than that, I was sorry that I'd never told her I loved her.

"One minute," said the *Muse*.

I suddenly wondered if this was the time the *Muse* had mentioned, through the dragoman, when I should bring Aglaé to the blue sphere with me when—how had she put it?—we should come there when it was our turn, before we act.

No, it didn't seem that this was what the *Muse* had meant. And it looked as if "our turn," whatever that might have been, would now never come.

The outer sphere filled all viewstrips. We could clearly see the dark undersides of continents and make out the actual turning of the sphere itself. To give us some sense of scale, the *Muse* superimposed an outline of the large continent on 25–25–261B against one of the smaller continents now on the top viewstrip. It was a tiny dot on the huge landmass.

Jaws dropped open but still no one spoke.

"Ten seconds to impact," the *Muse* said calmly. Our speed became apparent as we hurtled at the airless wall ahead of us—a wall that now seemed *flat* because it extended so far in each direction.

We struck.

We did not strike, actually, but passed through the seemingly solid underside, passed through a mile or two of ocean in a blink of an eye, passed through five or eight miles of blue-sky atmosphere above that, and then we were in space again, hurtling toward the next sphere— the eleventh celestial sphere according to the *Muse*'s earlier description, one a mere eighty-nine AU out from this impossible blue-white sun.

"We shed twenty-five percent of our velocity," the *Muse* reported.

"We couldn't...that's not...how could we..." stammered Tooley. "I mean—Abraxas's teeth!—even if the sphere floor were porous, impact with the ocean and atmosphere would have been...I mean...slowing twenty-five percent from..."

"Yes," agreed the *Muse*, "what we just experienced was not possible. We could not have survived. Such a deceleration could not have occurred. That much kinetic energy could not have been dissipated without much violence. Nine minutes until impact with the next sphere."

Thus we passed through the eleventh sphere at eighty-nine AU, and then the tenth at fifty-five AU—although the *Muse* informed us that it should be taking us many weeks to be covering these distances, even at our velocity still some double-digit percentage of light itself, and she suggested that time itself was out of joint in and around the ship, but we did not care about that—and then we approached the ninth sphere rotating at thirty-four AU from the blue-white star.

The *Muse of Fire* bored through an ocean just as the first three times—with Tooley muttering "hypercavitation" to himself as if the word meant anything—but this time we did not tear through the atmosphere and into space again.

The *Muse* rose slowly, reached the top of her arc, hung there a minute like a balloon hovering several thousand feet above a great, almost-but-not-quite flat expanse of green fields and forests and brown mountains, and then began to fall.

The *Muse* fired her engine almost gently. We passed over a coastline and then over wide plains toward a range of mountains.

"We are to land on that mesa," said the dragoman.

"Who's ordering us to land there?" demanded Kemp. "The Poimen?"

The dragoman smiled again and shook his head.

THE ARCHONS WERE the petty rulers according to our Gnostic faith, the Poimen the shepherds (although the gospels never told us *what* or *who* they were shepherds of), the *Demiurgos* were the architects, the fashioners, the true (but flawed and failed) creators of our world and universe, and Abraxas was God of All Opposites, Satan and Savior, Love and Hatred, and all other truths combined.

Now, as we all stood outside our ship in the sweet, rich air of this ninth-sphere world, the *Demiurgos* approached from the direction that might have been north.

None of us had ever set foot on a world as beautiful as this. From our mesa we could see hundreds if not thousands of square miles of green grasslands, rolling fields golden as if from wheat, thousands of acres of distant tidy orchards, more thousands of acres of apparently wild forest stretching off to the green foothills of a long mountain range, snow on the mountain peaks, a wide blue sky interrupted here and there by bands of clouds with some of the cumulonimbus rising ten miles into the blue sky, rain visibly falling in brushstroke dark bands far to our right, and more, a hint of our just-traversed coastline and ocean far, far to what we decided was the west, and from every direction the sweet scent of grass, growing things, fresh air, rain, blossoms, amid life.

"Is this Heaven?" Condella asked the dragoman.

"Why do you ask me?" was the naked dragoman's reply. He added a shrug.

That was when three *Demiurgos* approached from the north.

We'd already seen living things during our minutes alone on the mesa top—huge white birds in the distance, four-legged grazers that might have been Earth antelope or deer or wildebeest running in small herds many miles below on the great green sea of grass surrounding the mesa, large gray shadows in the faraway forests—elephants? rhinoceroses? dinosaurs? giraffes? any of Earth's long-extinct large wild things?

We hadn't brought binoculars out and couldn't tell without going back into the *Muse* to use her optics and now we didn't care as the *Demiurgos* approached.

We never doubted that these three were from the race of our Creators, even though no image of our Demiurge or his species appeared in our gospels or church windows.

They were six or seven hundred feet tall—above our height of three or four hundred feet above the lowlands here on the flat-topped mesa even though the bottoms of their legs were on the grasslands. They did not seem too massive for all their height because two thirds of each of them was in the form of three long, multiply articulated legs, each glowing a sort of metallic red and banded with black and dark blue markings, the three legs meeting in an almost artificial-looking metal-studded triangular disk of a torso—like a huge milking stool with living legs, was Tooley's later description.

It was the last hundred feet or so of *Demiurgos* that rose above the three legs and triangular torso that caught our attention.

Imagine a twenty-story-tall chambered nautilus rising from that metallic torso—not something *like* a chambered nautilus, but an actual shell—three shells here, each with its characteristic bright stripes—and from the lower opening of each spiraled shell, the living *Demiurgos* itself.

At the center of each shell was the circular umbilicus. Forward of that, over the massive opening, was a huge hood the color of dried blood. Beneath that hood on each side were the huge, perfectly round yellow eyes. Each black pupil at the center of each eye was large enough to have swallowed me.

And the word "swallow" did come to mind as the three *Demiurgos* tripoded their way closer until they hung over us; the great opening at the front of each shell was a mass of tentacles, tentacle sheaths, orangish-red spotted tonguelike material, horned funnels, and sphinctured apertures that might have been multiple mouths. Each huge yellow eye had its own long, fleshy ocular tentacle with a red-yellow node on its eye-end looking like some gigantic infested sty.

These were our Creators. Or at least one of them had been some twelve to twenty billion years ago. For

Creators, I thought, they were very fleshy and organic created things themselves, for all the beauty of their huge spiraled nautilus shells.

We'd all stepped back closer to the open airlocks and ports of the *Muse*, but none of us ran inside to hide. Not yet. I was painfully aware that the *Demiurgos* closest to me could whip down one of those sticky tongue-tentacles and have me in its bony funneled orifice in a second.

"You will perform a play now," said the dragoman. "The best one you know. Perform it well."

Kemp tore his gaze away from the gigantic tripods looming over us and to the dragoman, "You're in touch with them? They're speaking to you?"

The dragoman did not respond.

"Why won't they speak to *us*?" cried Burbank. "Tell them that we want talk to them, not perform another play."

"You will perform the best play you know now," said the dragoman, his voice flat in that way it got when he was channeling these other beings. "You will perform it to the best of your ability."

"Is this a test?" asked Aglaé. "At least ask them if this is a test."

"Yes," said the dragoman.

"Yes it's a test?" demanded Kemp.

"Yes."

"Why?" said Burbank.

The dragoman's large eyes were almost closed. The *Demiurgos's* huge yellow eyes above us never blinked but their ocular tentacles moved in a way that seemed hungry to me.

"What happens if we fail?" asked Aglaé.

"Your species will be extinguished," said the dragoman.

There was a roar of confused noise from all of us at that. The *Demiurgos* leaned farther over the mesa, their mouths and tentacles and eyes coming closer, and I picked up the strong brackish scent of the ocean—salt and reeking mud tidal flats and dead fish in the sun. I had a strong urge to run up the ramp into the *Muse* and hide in my bunk.

"That's just not...fucking...fair," Kemp said at last, speaking for all of us.

The dragoman smiled and I admit that I wouldn't have minded beating him to death at that moment. He spoke slowly, clearly: "Your species was excused upon first encounter because of Shakespeare. Only because of Shakespeare. His words and the meaning behind his words could not be fully comprehended, even unto the level of the Demiurge who created you. In your world, then, man was Abraxas—you gave birth to and devoured your own worlds and words, embracing eternal weakness even while you blazed with absolute creative power. You sought to build a bridge over death itself. All higher powers beneath the Absence that is Abraxas—the lowly Archons, the preoccupied Poimen, the race of *Demiurgos* themselves—voted that immediate extinction had to be your species' fate. But because of this one dead mind, this Shakespeare, there was a stay of execution on this sentence not to exceed one thousand and nine of your years. That time is up."

We stood silent in the sunlight. There was the sound in my ears of a single, huge, pounding heart, like the surf of a rising sea; I did not know if the pounding beat came from the *Demiurgos* whose shadow fell over me or from me.

"You will perform the best play that you know," repeated the dragoman. "And you will perform it to the best of your ability."

We looked at each other again. Finally Kemp said, *"Hamlet."*

THE SHOW WENT on. It took us half an hour to get into costumes, review roles—although we all knew our roles for *Hamlet* without asking—and slap on makeup, although the idea of the *Demiurgos* noticing our makeup was absurd. Then again, those huge, unblinking yellow eyes did not seem to miss anything, even though they stared through their own waving mass of tentacles when looking forward.

I was Rosenkrantz when we performed *Hamlet* and I enjoyed the part. Philp was Guildenstern. Old Adam had once told us that on Earth, pre-Contact, there had been a derivative play—not by Shakespeare supposedly—which featured Rosenkrantz and Guildenstern, those two lying but playful betrayers. I would have loved seeing it, if it ever did exist. Hell, I would have loved starring in it.

The other parts fell the way you would expect now that you know our troupe—Alleyn as Hamlet, Old Adam as Hamlet's father's ghost (a role our lore says the Bard himself sometimes played), Aglaé as Ophelia, Kemp as Claudius, Burbank as Polonius, Goeke as Horatio, Condella as Hamlet's mother Gertrude, Hywo as

Fortinbras...and so on. About the only profound talent in
our troupe not fully used in *Hamlet* was Heminges, who
carried *Othello* with his powerful Iago, cast as the gravedigger. Now the gravedigger—the official name in our
"Persons of the Play" list is "First Clown," the "Second
Clown" being the gravedigger's companion played today
by Gough—is one of the great roles in all of Shakespeare,
but it is relatively brief. Too brief for Heminges's ego.
But he made none of his usual protests this time as we
rushed to dress and finish our makeup. He even smiled,
as if performing for the *Demiurgos* to decide whether
our species would be annihilated or not was what he had
always looked forward to.

NONE OF US had slept for...I'd lost track of the hours,
but seventy-two hours at least and I guessed many more
(transiting the Pleroma strangely affects either one's sense
of time or time itself)...and we'd performed four daunting
plays: *Much Ado About Nothing* for the doles and arbeiters and late-coming Archons, *Macbeth*...shit, I mean "the
Scottish Play"...for the Archons, then *King Lear* for the
Poimen, and now *Hamlet*, a play that is almost impossible
to produce and act in well enough to do it justice at the
best of times. One critic, it is said, back in the pre-Contact
centuries, suggested that because of all the failed attempts
to put on *Hamlet*, we'd do better just to quit trying to
perform it and to allow everyone to read it.

Well, the *Demiurgos* did not look as if they were
waiting to be handed—tentacled?—copies of the script.

Under the brilliant yellow light of the distant blue-white star, the play went on. Waiting behind the arras with Philp for our characters to enter at the beginning of act 2, scene 2—Hamlet's fellow students and so-called friends confer and conspire with King Claudius and Queen Gertrude before going on to try to trick Hamlet into revealing what the royal couple wants know—I kept looking up and around.

This ninth sphere-world from the sun we were on was so large that we could not see the upward-curving horizons in any direction, merely a strange glowing haze that might have been the distance-distorted image of the inner wall rising up thousands of miles away from here. But I could see hints of the other eight spheres inward from us toward the sun. That was a sight I have no words for and perhaps Shakespeare would have failed here as well—the size, the crystalline clarity, the turnings within turnings, the shafts of sunlight and quick-caught glimpses of color that might have been continents and blue seas a solar system's leap away—but it made me cry.

I was doing a lot of crying on this trip. I'll blame it on the lack of sleep.

WHEN WE HAD thought our command performance for the Poimen was our last and ultimate test, Kemp and the others had chosen *King Lear* for a variety of reasons, but perhaps because *Lear*'s infinitudes and nihilisms are more manageable—by man or any species—than *Hamlet*'s ever-expanding paradoxes.

I've seen the play a hundred times and performed in it, usually as Rosenkrantz, more than half that number of times, but it always knocks me on my ass.

In all of Shakespeare's other plays, the characters that are larger than the play being performed—Falstaff, Rosalind, Cleopatra, the night porter in the Scottish Play, Mercutio—are either killed off or contained before they escape the deliberately confined double-sphered space of the play and theater. Not so with Hamlet and *Hamlet*. The play is *about* theater, not revenge, and is both the ultimate experience of theater and the ultimate comment on theater, and the strangely expanding consciousness of Hamlet—who begins as a student character prince about twenty years old and, within a few weeks in the time of the play, ages to a wise man in his fifties at least—makes no pretense of following any story line other than Hamlet's wildly leaping thoughts.

I strutted and fretted my enjoyable moments on the stage. The *Muse's* cabiri bots still were not working (Tooley had found that all their organic parts were missing), so we extended the usual stage and acted on without lighting, which would have been redundant in the bright sunshine anyway—and tried to make our entrances and exits without looking up at the hovering shells and tentacle-mouths of the three *Demiurgos*.

My last scene was one that had been sometimes omitted in our shorter performances of the play—act 4, scene 4, where we encounter Fortinbras's army on our way to the sea to sail to England, where Guildenstern and I are supposed to deliver Hamlet up to his execution but, according to offstage events, Hamlet will steal King

Claudius's execution request and substitute Guildie's and my names instead, so presumably this is my swan song, and my last words to Alleyn...Hamlet...are "Will't please you go, my lord?" but Hamlet is pleased to stay and to give what I call his "even for an eggshell" soliloquy. It's especially odd, and I thought so this day under the shadow of the slowly shifting *Demiurgos*, that Hamlet seems to be praising Fortinbras, who is little more than a quarrelsome killing machine.

> *I see*
> *The imminent death of twenty thousand men*
> *That for a fantasy and trick of fame*
> *Go to their graves like beds, fight for a plot*
> *Whereon the numbers cannot try the cause,*
> *Which is not tomb enough and continent*
> *To hide the slain? O, from this time forth*
> *My thoughts be bloody or be nothing worth!*

In other words, Hamlet—the paragon of human consciousness and occasional conscience (although he showed little enough of that when he stabbed stupid-but-innocent Polonius through the arras curtain and announced to his mother that he was going to lug the guts to another room)—was praising bloody action in a thug's nature rather than his own sublime awareness of morality and mortality.

And then the thought hit me like a stab between the ribs—*Where the fuck is Heminges?*

STILL IN ROSENKRANTZ costume, I ran up the ramp into the *Muse* and began throwing open hull hatches and sliding down ladders without my feet touching the steps.

Heminges was right where I expected him to be, in the *Muse*'s tiny room, but I hadn't expected the heavy spade—the one the gravedigger was to use in his upcoming encounter with Hamlet—in his hands. He'd obviously already taken half a dozen swings at the *Muse*'s blue globe—the metaglass was chipped and a few hairline cracks already extended from the niche where the spade-blade had fallen—and he was winding up to take another overhand swing when I leaped at him.

Heminges was fueled by a fanatic's rage—I could see white froth at the corners of his open mouth—but I was heavier, stronger, and younger than the professional Iago. I grabbed the spade, we whirled, and I forced him back against the bulkhead, but not before I'd glimpsed the *Muse*...the physical *Muse*, whoever or whatever she was floating in the red halo of her own hair, her newly young breasts almost touching the metaglass directly beneath the spade's damage, her arms passively down by her naked hips, her palms forward, as if she were awaiting the next and final spade blow almost with anticipation.

Heminges and I lurched around the small compartment with the comic clumsiness of two grown men fighting each other to the death. All four of our hands were gripping the long spade handle chin-high between us. Neither of us spoke; both of us grunted. Heminges's breath smelled of the whiskey we synthesized and broke out only after a successful performance.

Finally my youth and terror-augmented strength—combined with a lucky knee applied briskly to his cod-pieced balls—turned the tide and I forced Heminges against the bulkhead again and then up, up, the spade handle under his chin, until his toes left the deck. He hung there close to helpless. One final concerted press forward and I'd crush his Adam's apple with the handle, or just choke the fucking fool to death.

Instead of smashing his larynx, I panted, "What are you *doing*?"

His eyes, already wide, grew as round as the drag-oman's but much madder. "I...break...the globe..." he panted, breathing whiskey fumes all over me, "and the fusion reactor goes critical. We...blow...those alien...cocksuckers...to hell."

"Bullshit," I said, dropping him so his feet hit the deck but not relenting the pressure of the spade handle against his throat. If I slammed it up under his chin, it would snap his neck. "Nothing can make the reactor explode. Tooley told me so."

He tried to shake his head but it only resulted in the spade handle rubbing more skin from his already red-dened neck. "*She*...told me...it would," he gasped. His staring eyes were looking over my shoulder.

I released the pressure and turned to look at the *Muse*, the spade now hefted loosely in my hands. "How did she tell you?" I asked Heminges without turning to look at him. He was no threat. He'd slid down the bulkhead and was sprawled on the deck, panting and wheezing.

"Through dreams," he managed at last. "She gets...into...my dreams. If the reactor goes critical, we can blow a hole in this *Demiurgos* sphere and all the air will rush out and..."

He stopped. He must have realized then how insane that idea sounded. As if the *Demiurgos*'s home—the ultimate Creation of the Creators—could be so easily damaged.

I did not speak to him then, but looked directly into the *Muse*'s blue eyes when I spoke. "Did you really tell him that? Did you really get into his dreams and tell him he could do this? If you can turn this ship...yourself... into a hydrogen bomb, you sure don't need this aging Iago to help you do it. What the fuck are you up to, woman?"

The *Muse* smiled sadly at me but no voice came from the speaker grills on the wall.

I turned back to Heminges, stood over him, and handed him the spade. "Claudius, Gertrude, and Laertes are almost finished with their scene," I said. "Gough will be going on with his pickaxe without you. He'd just fucking *love* to take your part and deliver your lines. He'd always thought he'd make a better First Clown than you. I doubt if the goddamned *Demiurgos* will notice that there's an assistant gravedigger missing."

It was as if I'd run thousands of amps of current directly into Heminges's ass. He leaped up, steadied himself on the spade, shot an angry look at the *Muse*, and clambered up the steps and out. Actors, I thought, are nothing if not predictable.

My hands empty now, I spent another long moment staring at the naked woman in the blue sphere. I said nothing. This time she did speak through intercom, her words echoing in the otherwise empty ship.

"That had to be done, Wilbr, or he would have found a real way to damage the ship in his vain attempt at revolution. This way, I would have been the only one injured."

I still stared and said nothing. *Injured?* The *Muse* had been dead for centuries, the solid illusion of her naked young body here notwithstanding.

"Do bring her down here, just the two of you and the dragoman, as soon we enter the Pleroma," said the *Muse*. Her lips did not move, of course, mouth did not open, but it was her voice.

I did not say, "Yes." I did not say, "Bring who?" I said nothing.

After a moment I turned my back, scrambled up the ladder, and went out into the sunlight to watch the end of the play.

I'M SORRY THAT I used the word "brilliant" and perhaps even "unprecedented" when I described our performance of *King Lear* earlier...and perhaps I even used words like that to describe our performance of the Scottish Play in front of the Archon, or maybe (although I doubt it) our staging of *Much Ado About Nothing* for the arbeiters and doles the day before...because now I have no adequate words to describe the *truly brilliant* performance our people achieved with this *Hamlet*. I'd missed a few minutes, to be sure, wrestling with Heminges and the spade down in the storm cellar of the *Muse*, but I'd not missed so much that I didn't realize how truly extraordinary this show had been. Whoever the long-dead critic had been, if he'd been real at all, who said that *Hamlet* should be read rather than seen to be fully appreciated...well, he hadn't seen *this* performance.

Our people were half dead with exhaustion and tension by the last line, but somehow that added to the verisimilitude and unique quality of the performance. It was as if we had *lived* these hours—eternities—with the Prince of Denmark and his wit. Even those who hadn't acted or who had simply been onstage as placeholders—the soldiers, attendants, guards, messengers, sailors, followers of Laertes and so forth—seemed as totally wrung out as Alleyn, Aglaé, Kemp, and the other principals.

Heminges, I should mention, was goddamned wonderful. He's the only character in the play—a play in which even the most inconsequential character speaks more artfully than any man or woman now alive—who is a worthy interlocutor to Hamlet. If language is a game—and when is it not with Shakespeare?—then the grave-digger was the only player who should have been allowed on the court with the fiendishly witty Hamlet. "'Tis a quick lie, sir, 'twill away again from me to you," the gravedigger says once, taking one of Hamlet's serves and smashing it back across the net. (We know about tennis through *Henry V*.)

Even before they are fully engaged in their battle of wits, Hamlet says of the gravedigger to Horatio, "How absolute the knave is. We must speak by the card or equivocation will undo us." Burbank taught me that this is a sailor's card, a shipman's card, that Hamlet is referring to—one on which all thirty-two compass points are clearly marked.

But *Hamlet* is a play in which no clear compass points have ever been marked to guide either the actors or the audiences. It ends, as Hamlet himself does, with far more brilliant questions asked than answered. When Hywo as Fortinbras, his voice husky with exhaustion and emotion, speaks the last words of the play over our rough stage strewn with corpses.

> *Take up the bodes. Such a sight as this*
> *Becomes the field, but here shows much amiss.*
> *Go, bid the soldiers shoot.*

And all the living exited by march, carrying Hamlet's body with them; we did not provide the sound effects of the cannon shooting as we usually did.

There was only silence: a silence broken only by the gentle afternoon breezes blowing across the mesa and the slight creakings and stirring of the *Demiurgos*'s triple legs and metal girdles and many tentacles. Their great yellow eyes did not blink. It was as if they were waiting for an encore.

Our dead sat up onstage. We actors, including Alleyn who was almost staggering from exhaustion and Aglaé, who was as pale as the real drowned Ophelia, came back onstage, joined hands, and bowed.

The *Demiurgos* made no sound or new movement.

"Well," said Kemp at last, still wearing the dead Claudius's crown as he faced the silent dragoman. "Did we pass? Does the human race continue? What's our grade?"

"You are to return to your ship and seal it," said the dragoman.

"Fuck that!" cried Kemp. He was shouting now at the looming ship-sized shells of the *Demiurgos*, I noticed, not at the round-eyed dragoman. "Give us your answer. Give us your verdict. We've done our bleeding best for every race of you alien pricks. Tell us *now*."

"You are to return to your ship and seal it," repeated the dragoman.

"Arrrrrhh!" screamed Kemp and threw his crown at the tentacled maw of the nearest Demiurge. It did not quite make contact.

We all went into the ship. The hatches were sealed. The viewstrips showed the *Demiurgos* ambling away to the north in their long three-legged strides in the short minute before the mesa rock and grass beneath the ship glowed white, then yellow, then turned into a long metallic funnel, and the ship fell—or was flung—violently down and down and then out. The internal fields all kicked on and we were frozen in place as the *Muse* compensated for the deadly acceleration gravities assailing us. Evidently they were within the thirty-one g's she could handle. A moment later we abruptly transited to the gold nothingness of the Pleroma—the *Demiurgos* had not even bothered flinging us out through their tenth, eleventh, and twelfth spheres before making the transit leap—and Kemp said, "I'll interpret our being allowed to leave as a passing grade."

"Allowed to leave?" said Heminges. "They fucking well booted us out."

Burbank said, "I'm going to get some sleep," and everyone cheered raggedly and we began to head for our bunks. Some were so exhausted that they fell on couches or the deck and were instantly asleep.

I sought out Aglaé before she disappeared up to her bunk cubbie.

⤞

"Do you trust me?" I asked when I'd asked her to follow me down to the *Muse*'s level and she'd grudgingly complied. It felt strange to be alone with Aglaé in the dim blue light with the naked female form floating just a few feet away.

"Do you trust me?" I asked again when she did not reply immediately.

"Wilbr, what do you want? I'm tired. Very tired." She had every right to be, I realized. Aglaé had held important parts in all four plays we'd presented in the last three endless, continuous, sleepless days and nights of strangeness. "If you brought me down here for..." she began with a warning in her voice.

We were interrupted by the dragoman coming down the ladder after dogging the overhead hatch behind him. I'd not told him to come.

I turned to the *Muse* in her sphere. The tiny cracks where the spade had dented the surface had not spread. My guess was that the metaglass would have survived a thousand spade attacks. "We're here," I said to the naked form.

"In immeasurable distance there glimmers a solitary star on the highest point of heaven," said the dragoman in the *Muse*'s voice, accurate down to her new youthful energy. "This is the only God of this lonely star. This is his world, his Pleroma, his divinity."

I knew the words so well I could have recited them myself. Any of us could have. This was from Saint Jung's Seventh Sermon to the Dead.

"There is nothing that can separate man from his own God, if man can only turn his gaze away from the fiery spectacle of Abraxas," continued the *Muse*'s voice through the dragoman's mouth. I understood that she was communicating with us this way so the rest of the ship would not hear. But why? Why this sermon?

Aglaé looked at me with growing concern in her eyes. She didn't like this sermon coming from the ship's soul, and neither did I. I shook my head to show her my own confusion.

"Man here," said the *Muse*. This was the penultimate verse of the Seventh Sermon, word for word. "God there. Weakness and insignificance here, eternal creative power there. Here is but darkness and damp cold. There all is sunshine."

"*Muse*," began Aglaé, "why have you—"

"Upon hearing this, the dead fell silent," continued the *Muse* as if Aglaé had not spoken, "and they rose up like smoke rises over the fire of the shepherd, who guards his flock by night."

"Amen," Aglaé and I said in unison, out of habit.

"Anagramma," said the *Muse,* her voice lower, completing the Seventh Sermon with its sacred and secret codicil. "Nahtriheccunde. Gahinneverahtunin. Zehgessurklach. Zunnus."

Alarm klaxons began blaring throughout the ship. More alarms rang and bleated and thumped. The *Muse*'s voice—her old voice, probably a recorded voice, her voice in rare alarm even as her face behind the metaglass stayed serene, her eyes watchful—shouted out, "Warning! Warning! The airlocks are opening! The airlocks are opening! We are in Pleroma and all hatches and airlocks are opening! Warning!"

At that moment the dragoman's neurofiber filaments slipped through my skin and flesh and pierced the nerves at the base of my skull. I saw filaments wrapping around Aglaé's lovely neck and doing the same. More filaments shot forward from the dragoman's head, made contact with the metaglass, and then passed through. The *Muse* extended her body so that the filaments pierced her small, white breasts.

"Warning! Airlocks opening. All hatches opening. We are in the Pleroma. Warning! Air pressure dropping. Don protective gear. Warning! All airlocks are..." came the recorded voice at full volume from all speakers, but the words grew tinier and tinnier and then disappeared completely as the last air roared and hissed and flowed out of the ship through all of its open airlocks and hatches and doors, while the golden vacuum of the Pleroma flowed in to each compartment and all of our straining lungs with its nothingness.

"COME OUT!" COMMANDED the voice, but only Aglaé, the dragoman, and I could do so. The others might have been dead, their lungs and eyes and eardrums exploded. Or they could be frozen in the vacuum-thick Pleroma like ancient insects in amber. In either case, they could not move.

Aglaé and I could do so and we did, laboriously climbing the ladder, floating and swimming through the golden medium to the airlock, then out into the Abyss. It seemed to take centuries. But no one was in a hurry. The dragoman followed, his long spatulate fingers and flattened feet pulling him and pushing him through the golden nothing with easy, broad, flick-away swimming motions.

Abraxas was waiting outside. I was not surprised. I could feel that Aglaé was not surprised either, nor the *Muse*—who was watching us somehow, I felt, even though the external imagers no longer worked for those trapped inside.

When I say that we went—or swam—outside into the Abyss, the Pleroma, it gives no real sense of the experience. The Abyss or Void or Pleroma was not absence; it was Fullness beyond all measure. It filled our mouths and lungs and eyes and cells. Moving in it was a matter of will, not locomotion. Once outside, there was no up, no down, no side to side, Aglaé and I willed and swam our way through the golden fullness to the long, gray curve of the outer hull of the ship—the only thing, other than Abraxas and us, that fouled the ineffable absoluteness of the Pleroma. We could use the hull as down if we stood on it; as a wall if we set our backs against it or near it; as a ceiling if we so chose. It gave us reference. Everything else, other than Abraxas was waiting, was…ineffable.

I had learned that word in my catechisms as a child, but I never understood ineffable until this minute. Even as my mind reeled with vertigo, it remembered the words of our Gnostic prophet Basilides as quoted by Hippolytus some thousands of years before Contact ended all context.

For that which is really ineffable is not named Ineffable, but is superior to every name that is used...

Naught was, neither matter, nor substance, nor voidness of substance, nor simplicity, nor impossibility of composition, nor inconceptibility, nor imperceptibility, neither man, nor angel, nor god; in fine, neither anything at all for which man has ever found a name, nor any operation which falls within the range either of perception or conception. Such, or rather far more removed from the power of man's comprehension, was the state of nonbeing, when the Deity beyond being, without thinking, or felling, or determining, or choosing, or being compelled, or desiring, willed to create universality.

This pretty well defined the Pleroma that Aglaé and I found ourselves floating in: a field that was at once boundless, impersonal, indefinable, and absolutely transcendental. This was the *"Ain Soph Aur"* of the Jewish Kabbalah and the Tibetan and Mongolian and Buddhist "Eternal Parent, wrapped in her Ever-Invisible Robes, asleep in the Infinite Bosom of Duration."

And that pretty well described Abraxas as well.

The Abraxas who waited for us here, the incarnation He chose to show us, held no surprises. This Abraxas was the Heavenly Chanticleer, straight from the paintings in Gnostic churches throughout the Tell: small as far as manifested Absolute Gods go—only about six feet tall, a little shorter than me—and matching our images down to his rooster's head, curled serpent legs, and the whip he carried in one inhuman hand and the shield he carried in the other. The stars with their resplendent rays and the *ogdoad* symbol of the transcending seven planets were on his shield here rather than floating behind him, but the center of the large gold shield was taken up with a complicated design working the gold of the shield into the face of the sun. Abraxas's eyes were not those of a rooster, but rather the predator orbs of a lion. His mouth was mostly beak, but the teeth and tongue were also those of a lion.

All in all, a modest visible incarnation for the God of Totality, the Lord of Opposites, who not only stands outside of time but rules outside of all mere religions as the reality of the eternally available timeless moment.

"You will perform a play," said the dragoman.

"Yeah, yeah," I said. "What else is new?"

When I tell you "the dragoman said" or "I said," the words are not correct since the medium of the Pleroma, which was not a medium at all, carried no sound. There was no air in my lungs or in Aglaé's lungs. The Pleroma satisfied our brains' and cells' need for oxygen, but it was exactly as if we'd drowned in the Fullness. I know that the other twenty-one members of our troupe were writhing in terror in the ship, trying to move, trying to breathe air that was no longer there, no more concerned about performing a Shakespearean play than a fish out of water would have been about working out multiplication tables as it writhed and flopped on some hostile shore.

But something the *Muse* or the dragoman—or both—had done to Aglaé and me allowed us to think, to move, and, by shaping the words with our mouths and minds even in the golden absence of actual air, to shape our thoughts to be heard as speech.

"Will you perform?" asked the dragoman, presumably speaking for Abraxas who floated before us.

I looked at Aglaé. She nodded, but this was redundant. After whatever we had experienced in the *Muse*'s room, this young woman and I were as in tune as two tuning forks struck to the same pitch and vibration.

"We will do parts of *Romeo and Juliet*," I said. "However much we can as a troupe of two."

Now, neither Kemp nor Burbank nor any of the other elders of our troupe would have chosen *Romeo and Juliet* as one of Shakespeare's pieces to perform when the future of our species—or even an important performance—was at stake. As appreciated as the old standard was by arbeiter and dole audiences around the Tell—and by the troupe itself, to tell the truth—it was earlier, easier Shakespeare: brilliant in its parts, but never the incomparable artistic achievement that was *King Lear* or *Hamlet* or *Othello* or *The Tempest* or even the Scottish Play.

What were our choices? It would have made more sense to put on *The Tempest* before the God of the Sun and Darkness, dealing as it does with the ultimate magus, magic, enchanted islands, captured races turned into slaves, and the end of control, probably Shakespeare's farewell to the theater if Kemp in his cups is to be believed—literally the drowning of Prospero's Books.

But I couldn't have done Prospero on my best day. I'd never been understudy for Prospero and had had no regular role on the rare occasions when we produced it.

And however we might abridge *The Tempest,* it would never make a workable two-person production for Aglaé and me.

Of course, neither would *Romeo and Juliet*, but I regularly played Samson in the opening scenes—"No, sir, I do not bite my thumb at you, sir, but I bite my thumb, sir"—and I'd been understudy for Alleyn as Romeo on multiple occasions. And Aglaé was wonderful as Juliet.

And so we started.

We decided to use the hull as a sort of wall behind us, better to define the stage in our minds and to reach back to touch if the pleromic vertigo became too bad. Other than the absurd rooster-headed Abraxas—solitary King, Bond of Invisibility, Breaker of the Cycles of Bondage, and First Power—there wasn't anything to look at or hold on to out there in the Pleroma except the dragoman and the hull. And Aglaé.

I looked at her, nodded, and floated forward a few yards.

> *Two households, both alike in dignity,*
> *In fair Verona (where we lay our scene),*
> *From ancient grudge break to new mutiny,*
> *Where civil blood makes civil hands unclean.*
> *From forth the fatal loins of these two foes*
> *A pair of star-crossed lovers take their life;*
> *Whose misadventured piteous overthrows*
> *Doth with their death bury their parents' strife.*

Aglaé was watching me intently, wondering, I am sure, if I was going to do the entire Chorus's part, but

I wasn't sure of the last part so I broke off there. Then I raised my arms and said conversationally in the direction of Abraxas, who was now seated on a gold throne that had not been there a second before, "Imagine, if you will, two young men, Samson and Gregory, of the house of Capulet, entering in swords and bucklers."

Then I did act out all the parts between Samson and Gregory—I knew these lines well enough—and after that, quickly explaining the situation to the dragoman and the Lord of Light and Darkness in easily improvised phrases, I acted out the entrance of Abraham and a serving man of the House of Montague. In other words, I got to deliver my "but I bite my thumb, sir" line after all.

Aglaé had crossed her arms. I could read her thought. *Will you he doing Juliet as well?*

Instead I improvised a clumsy little summary of Montague and Benvolio's scene—I'd played Benvolio once before when Philp was ill—and then summarized the coming scene between Benvolio and Romeo, stepping into character when it came time for Romeo's major lines and speeches—he was smitten and love-sodden already, you remember—but, we learn, with Fair Rosaline, not Juliet. Shakespeare, never all that interested in logic or verisimilitude, was asking us to believe that in that small town where the Montagues and the Capulets had been entwined with enmity for centuries like a climbing vine on an ancient trellis, Romeo had somehow not seen, or even heard of, Juliet yet.

I stepped—or floated—back. Taking her cue perfectly, Aglaé moved forward facing Abraxas, summarized the scene with old Capulet, Paris, and the clown servingman

Peter in just a few words, and then launched into the scene where she played Capulet's wife, the inimitable Nurse, and Juliet herself. Aglae's voice was never so beautiful as when she spoke for Juliet—a girl-woman only thirteen years old in Shakespeare's mind. My Romeo was years younger than I in real life…"real life" being the mind of the Bard.

And so our play advanced.

For the next scene, I summarized Benvolio's parts but found that I could do most of Mercutio's amazing lines perfectly from memory. "If love be rough with you, be rough with love: Prick love for pricking, and you beat love down." I'd seen Mercutio performed by the best men of our troupe and now I added my own little bits of business with closed fist and thrust forearm for the pricking lines, picking up Mercutio's madness and Romeo's naïve responses without hesitating a nanosecond between the wide shifts in tone and voice and posture and mannerism.

All my life, I realized, I'd wanted to do the Queen Mab speech, and now I did, babbling on about the tiny fairies' midwife, her wagon's spokes made of spinners' legs, the cover, the wings of grasshoppers, her whip of cricket bone…faster and faster, madder and madder, a tortured young man with eloquence rivaling Shakespeare's but none of the solid, business side of the Bard; Mercutio, a man in love with his own words and willing to follow words where they led even as they led him to madness…

"'Peace, peace, Mercutio, peace! Thou talk'st of nothing,'" I interrupted myself in my Romeo voice, alarmed now at my much more brilliant friend's frenzy, shifting my body in space through three dimensions as if shaking the space where I'd stood as Mercutio an instant before.

And so the play slid forward in that timeless space-less space.

I realized almost at once that Aglaé was better at improvising the summaries than I—and she could remember most of the other players' lines and Chorus's long speeches word for word when she wanted to retrieve any of them—so I let her take the lead, only stepping in as Romeo or Mercutio or Tybalt for key lines, and then only a few. It was as if we were skipping across the surface of a pond, saving ourselves from falling in only through speed and unwillingness to fall and drown.

Then it was our first encounter, our first scene together as our real characters, all thoughts of Rosaline out of my teenaged mind now, my heart and soul and stirring prick focused forever more on the transcendent image of Juliet—

"O she doth teach the torches to burn bright!"

We asked the unmoving Abraxas to imagine the party, Tybalt's anger, Capulet's restraint of the young fire-brand, the singing, the dancing, the men and women in bright colors and masks, and all the while young Romeo following, almost stalking, young Juliet. Our banter had the urgency of youth and love and lust and of the reality—shared by so few in all of time!—of truly having found the one person in the cosmos meant for you.

"'Good pilgrim, you do wrong your hand too much,'" whispered Juliet/Aglaé. "'Which mannerly devotion shows in this…'"

A second later I leaned close to her. "'Have not saints lips, and holy palmers, too?'"

"'Ay, pilgrim, lips that they must use in prayer.'"

" 'O then, dear saint, let lips do what hands do. They… pray.' " And I sent my palm against hers and we both pressed hard. " 'Grant thou, lest faith turn to despair.' "

When we did kiss a few seconds later, it was—for both of us, I could feel—unlike any kiss or physical experience either of us had ever known. It lasted a very long time. I touched her thoughts as well as her lips. Her trust—never fully given before, I understood at that instant, chased by so many men, stolen by a few, betrayed by all others—opened warmly around me.

She floated above me during the balcony scene. It was the first time I'd ever understood the depth and youthful shallowness and hope in those lines I'd heard too many times before.

I was Mercutio and Benvolio and Romeo in coming scenes, even while Aglaé delivered selected lines from the Nurse and from Peter.

She summarized Friar Lawrence's part except for certain responses to her Juliet.

Suddenly I found myself acting out Mercutio's verbal taunts with Tybalt, Benvolio's failed attempts to intervene, Romeo's joyful interruption, the mock fight between Tybalt and Mercutio that led to Mercutio being slain under Romeo's arm.

To an observer—and in a real sense Abraxas was the only observer, since the dragoman's eyes and ears were presumably just conduits to Him—it must have looked as if I were having an epileptic fit in freefall, babbling at myself, twisting, floating, lunging with invisible épées, moaning, dying. "They have made worms' meat of me," cries Mercutio.

"O!" cries Romeo. "I am fortune's fool."

IN ACT 3, scene 5, Aglaé and I made love. We actually made love.

We had not intended to do it, even as our thoughts flew between us like messenger doves during the intimacy of our almost perfect improv. *I* had not thought of doing it.

But as the scene opens but before Juliet says "Wilt thou be gone? It is not yet near day," our stage directions say only that we are both aloft, with a ladder of cords, but Kemp had often staged it with Romeo and Juliet half-dressed on a couch standing in for their marriage bed. Offstage, of course, between scenes, had been Romeo and Juliet's one night of bliss as man and wife—a very few hours of realized love before the lark pierced the fearful hollow of their ears and never, as fate would have it, to be followed by another night or moment of intimacy.

But before Aglaé spoke that first line—she hesitated, her eyes on mine, the God and dragoman forgotten by both of us—I began to undress her. She rushed to undress me.

But the lovemaking was not rushed. I have no need to describe it here and you have no need to hear details, but trust me that there was nothing rushed, nothing self-conscious, no sense of doom or finality, no awareness of other eyes on us—neither divine nor dragomanic—and we made love as joyously and slowly and then as impetuously and wildly as Romeo and Juliet would have at their age and in their depths of first-love rapture.

I did love her. Juliet. Aglaé. My love. My life.

We half-dressed afterward, she delivered her "Wilt thou be gone?" line, we laughed and debated whether it was the lark or the nightingale—the former meant death to me from Juliet's family, but I laughed out, " 'Let me be ta'en, let me be put to death. I am content, so thou wilt have it so.' "

That wakens her to the morn and danger. She all but shoves me out with protests and final kisses and more final hugs and kisses.

I'd forgotten Abraxas. Forgotten the floating dragoman with the unblinking eyes. I'd forgotten everything but my performance and the truth beneath it—which was my body still vibrating like a struck bell because of my lovemaking with Aglaé and the knowledge that should the human race or universe itself end tomorrow, it was all worth it for these moments.

It was in our final tomb scene together that I realized that we were probably going to die then and there.

Our lovemaking had been spontaneous but real.

Our love was new but real.

The lines we were delivering had never been delivered like this by living actors in all the history of time or theater. Our energies were absolute. Our emotions all real.

I was sure that when I pantomimed drinking the poison in Juliet's tomb, I would feel the cold spread of the true apothecary's poison actually move through my veins like death-ice. And then, a moment later, when Aglaé pantomimed my dagger entering her breast, real blood would flow into the Pleroma and she would die.

"'Here's to my love,'" I whispered anyway, holding up the imaginary bottle and drinking it all down. "'O true apothecary. Thy drugs are quick. Thus with a kiss I die.'"

The kiss was brief. I was dying after all. I fell, floating slowly away from where she floated horizontally in the golden glow.

I did not die. Nor did Aglaé's make-believe dagger pierce an all-too-real and beating heart. The show went on. I summarized Friar Lawrence's lines, the Page's, the Watchman's, then Aglaé reported Capulet's wife's and Montague's sorrow in snippets of dialogue, and then I delivered Balthasar's and the Prince's important lines.

Aglaé floated dead again while I boomed out in a prince's royal voice.

A glooming peace this morning with it brings,
The sun for sorrow will not show his head.
Go hence to have more talk of these sad things;
Some shall be pardoned, and some punishèd:
For never was a story of more woe
Than this of Juliet and her Romeo.

Aglaé floated upright next to me and took my hand. We bowed together in Abraxas's direction.

The God who was also the Devil, the apotheosis of Night and Day combined, did not move. His rooster eyes did not blink. His arms on the throne were still. His serpent legs with their serpent heads and fangs and serpent eyes did not stir or slither.

Aglaé and I looked to the dragoman.

Time did not move in this timeless place, but I could feel Aglaé's heartbeats and my own. We lived.

"Well?" I said to the dragoman at last.

"Return to your ship," he said.

"Not yet," I said. Aglaé and I kicked forward together, floating closer to the throne and the God above Gods seated on it. We could clearly see the lion teeth in the huge rooster beak as we came closer.

We stopped in front of Him. "Do you have anything to say to us?" I asked.

"Speak now," said Aglaé to the thing on the throne, "or forever hold your peace.

Abraxas did not stir or blink.

I raised my fist and brought it down hard on the God's head. The chanticleer coxcomb and skull cracked and fell away when I struck again.

Aglae's small fists pounded His chest. It also cracked and then opened, showing hollowness inside.

The Unlikely Likely One, the All-Powerful in the Realms of Reality and Unreality was as hollow and fragile as a plaster statue.

We turned to look at the dragoman.

"It's always been you," said Aglaé.

"Of course," said the naked form. "Let's get back into the *Muse* before you catch your death of cold out here."

THE *MUSE* SEALED the airlocks, pumped the Pleroma out, released real air into the ship from storage tanks, and the twenty-one other members of troupe began gasping and gagging and coughing and retching. All had survived.

"There have been alterations," came the *Muse*'s voice through the intercoms. "I can transit the Pleroma on my own now. To anywhere in the Tell beyond. Where would you have us go?"

Without really thinking or waiting for Kemp or Burbank or Condella or others—even my beloved Aglaé—to respond, I said, "25–25–261B."

This transit took less than thirty minutes.

As much as we all wanted to crawl to our bunks and sleep for a month, most of us showered and dressed in our clean ship tunics and gathered in the common room, where Kemp and other older ones—still thinking they commanded the ship or their destinies—demanded to know what had happened in the Pleroma. I let Aglaé tell them.

"What was Abraxas's verdict then?" asked Heminges. "On whether the human race continues or ends?" Aglaé had left out the part where we had found our God to be brittle, dead, false, and hollow.

"Perhaps we'll see on 25–25–261B," I said just as the *Muse* announced that we had exited the Pleroma and were approaching the planet.

The *Muse* roared down through cloud and sky on her thundering three-mile-long pillar of fire. It was daytime and the hot winds were howling in from the high desert above the arbeiters' and doles' plateau.

We suited up in hot condition suits and filter masks and went out anyway.

What we'd seen from orbit was true: the arbeiter barracks were empty, the dole hovels and offices deserted, the mushroom mine works abandoned and silent except for the howling of the wind.

Everyone was gone.

We returned to the ship and I ordered it to rise and hover near the Archon keep.

The stone-steel walls were there, but only a shell now. It looked as if a great fire had consumed every part of the interior. Embers still glowed.

"Where is everyone?" I asked the dragoman.

He showed spatulate fingers in an openhanded gesture even while he gave his small-shouldered shrug. "Perhaps the Archons have gone home—"

"I don't mean the goddamned Archons," I interrupted. "I mean the people. The human beings. The slaves. The people."

If he had shrugged again, or smiled, I would have killed him then—be he dragoman or divinity or both—but he only said, "Perhaps you failed your tests and your people are no more. Gone from the galaxy, with your troupe soon to follow."

"No," I said. It was not a protest, merely a statement of certainty.

"Then perhaps some...force...has removed them from all worlds in the Tell where they were in bondage and sent them home to Earth," he said.

I shook my head. "There's not room enough on Earth, even without the oceans, even if the goddamned tombs were to be torn down, for the billions upon billions of us from the Tell," I said.

"Then perhaps the oceans are being refilled and the... goddamned tombs...torn down as we speak," said the dragoman. "And perhaps your kind has been returned also to more Earthlike worlds—beyond the Tell, perhaps even among the Spheres, where they can resume their stumble toward their destiny."

"What in the hell is this...*thing*...babbling about?" demanded Kemp.

"This *thing* is more God than Abraxas or the Poimen or the Archons were or will ever be," I said tiredly.

Kemp and the others could only stare with their mouths open. I think all of our mouths were open. We were all learning to breathe air again.

"It was never really a test of *us*, was it?" I asked the dragoman.

"Only in the sense that every one of your performances is always a test," he said.

"But you were testing *them*," I said. "The Archons. The Poimen. The *Demiurgos*. Even Abraxas, if there is such a thing."

"Yes," said the dragoman. "There is no Abraxas, but there are the Abraxi. They *are* the Pleroma. Think of them as a sort of primal cosmic zooplankton. They are not very intelligent and make piss-poor gods."

"Did all these species pass?" I asked.

"Not all of them." The dragoman walked past us and looked at the Archon keep a mile below us. "Do you want that to remain?" he asked.

"No," I said. While the others were trying to understand what we were talking about, I said to the *Muse*, "Full fusion thrust, please. Melt that place to slag."

The *Muse* did what I asked. We felt the internal fields press around us as the ship leaped back into space.

"Were you really dead?" I asked the dragoman. "Did the Poimen really resurrect you from the dead?"

"I was. They thought they did. I have allowed others to believe the same in other places and at other times. Illusions are important for children, especially illusions about oneself or one's place in the universe."

"Do they know who you are? What you are?"

"No," said the dragoman. He showed his thin, lipless smile again. "Do you?"

Before I could speak—and I do not know to this day what I was about to say—the dragoman said to us all, "You will encounter hundreds of other races of sentient and tool-using, if not always intelligent, beings if you cross the Pleroma to places beyond the Tell. None of them are gods. You will have war with some if you want to survive. Some may have to die out. Some will want to destroy you. Some you may wish to destroy or conquer. You will have to look inside yourselves and to your poetry when those choices are faced."

Aglaé said, "So there are no gods out there?"

"None out there," said the dragoman. "Perhaps one or more in here." He disappeared and we all leaped back as the air rushing into the space where he had been made a small thunderclap.

The *Muse's* sudden voice from the walls made us all jump again.

Were all stars to disappear or die,
I should learn to look at an empty sky
And feel its total dark sublime,
Though this might take me a little time.

"Which of the Bard's plays is that from?" asked Burbank, his voice hoarse with exhaustion and disbelief that there were lines he did not know.

"It's not Shakespeare," replied the *Muse* in her new, young voice so filled with dark energy. "It's by a man named Wystan Hugh Auden. You people need to learn some new poets."

"Perhaps you'll have time to teach us," I said. "Where are we now, please?" The viewstrips showed only stars, darkness, and arcane coordinates.

"We're approaching pleromic transit-phase velocity," said the *Muse*. "What is your desired destination?"

Only Aglaé spoke, but she spoke for all of us.

"Home."